Abdel D. Streight, Pres. of the United States

The Crisis of Eighteen Hundred and Sixty-One in the Government of the United States

Its cause, and how it should be met. Containing the celebrated

proclamation of Andrew Jackson to the South Carolina nullifiers

Abdel D. Streight, Pres. of the United States

The Crisis of Eighteen Hundred and Sixty-One in the Government of the United States
Its cause, and how it should be met. Containing the celebrated proclamation of Andrew Jackson to the South Carolina nullifiers

ISBN/EAN: 9783337378448

Printed in Europe, USA, Canada, Australia, Japan

Cover: Foto ©Andreas Hilbeck / pixelio.de

More available books at **www.hansebooks.com**

THE CRISIS

OF

EIGHTEEN HUNDRED AND SIXTY-ONE

IN THE GOVERNMENT OF THE

UNITED STATES.

ITS CAUSE,

AND HOW IT SHOULD BE MET.

CONTAINING THE CELEBRATED PROCLAMATION OF ANDREW
JACKSON TO THE SOUTH CAROLINA NULLIFIERS; WEB-
STER'S ANSWER TO HAYNE ON THE SUBJECT OF
NULLIFICATION, AND SEVERAL EXTRACTS
FROM LETTERS WRITTEN BY JOHN JAY,
JAMES MADISON, AND ALEXANDER
HAMILTON, PENDING THE ADOP-
TION OF THE CONSTITU-
TION.

BY A. D. STREIGHT.

INDIANAPOLIS, IND.:
PUBLISHED BY THE AUTHOR.
1861.

CONTENTS.

TO THE FLAG OF OUR UNION,

TO THE MEMORY OF THE IMMORTAL HEROES,

WHO ESTABLISHED IT,

AND TO THE TRUE HEARTED PATRIOTS,

WHO WILL MAINTAIN IT,

THIS VOLUME IS MOST RESPECTFULLY DEDICATED,

BY THE AUTHOR.

PREFACE.

In presenting this volume to the people, we shall offer no apology. It has been our constant effort to condense into as small a compass as possible our views relative to the cause of our nation's calamity, and the proper course to be pursued to restore the supremacy of the laws, the integrity of the constitution, and to preserve the Union. We have aimed at nothing but the good of our distracted country. That some will differ with us relative to our proposed plan of managing our national affairs in this hour of peril, is no more than we expect. We are aware that there are true-hearted and well-meaning men who are of the opinion that we had better compromise with the traitors to our country than to use forcible means to compel obedience to the laws. But we think they are seriously mistaken; that such a measure will but produce a temporary calm that will be succeeded by a storm of increased violence. We have labored in the first place to show that our present troubles are owing to a mistaken policy on the part of our government in adopting temporary pacification measures, instead of maintaining the supremacy of the laws. We have also endeavored to show from letters written by some of the founders of our government, that this is a government of the people collectly, and not a government of the States. We have further endeavored to show that the wisest of our statesmen were in favor of enforcing the laws regardless of the feelings of those who rebelled against them; and finally, we trust, that we have shown that a Republican government cannot be maintained unless the people of every section of the country are compelled to submit to the constitutional acts of the majority. We wish our Southern brethren no harm, but they *must* learn that this is a government composed of freemen who will submit to their dictation no longer; and the sooner they are apprized of this fact the better it will be for all parties concerned. The necessity for a work of this kind has caused us to lay aside most pressing business matters which needed our attention; but in these perilous times we feel it our duty to do all we can to unite the people upon this momentous crisis in our national affairs. The hurried manner in which this work has been prepared. will account for the imperfections.

A. D. STREIGHT.

THE CRISIS.

WHAT PRODUCED IT.

When we behold a blooming youth, just entering upon the sphere of manhood, the fondest hopes of his honored parents, the admiration of all who know him, the brightest genious of his age, begin to wither and decay, our sinking spirits are aroused to make deep, anxious, earnest enquiry as to the nature and cause of the disease that threatens to drag him to an untimely grave, and bring misery, sorrow and pain to his unhappy parents, friends and admirers, and if there is to be found a remedy within the knowledge of man that will remove the malady, we are wont to apply it with the utmost promptitude, and await its effects with fearful apprehensions and the deepest suspense. No time is lost or exertion spared by the friends of the afflicted, but with a united effort they rally, each anxious to contribute the utmost of his ability to rescue the unfortunate sufferer from the dangers that threaten to rob them of one to whom they feel bound by every endearing tie that binds mankind to earth. Now, while a case like this should justly excite our sympathies and awaken every principle of humanity dwelling in the heart, yet how unimportant and insignificant is such a case, when compared with the decaying symptoms of a great, free, powerful and prosperous nation of over thirty millions of inhabitants, whose institutions have been the hope and pride of the friends of liberty, whose prosperity is the marvel of the world, whose commerce extends to the most remote portions of the earth, whose territory covers twenty-three degrees of lattitude and sixty degrees of longitude, whose soil is unsurpassed for the variety and richness of its productions, whose government has been the shield and asylum for the oppressed of all nations, and whose prosperity and power has been the object of jealousy and dread of the tyrants of every division of the globe. Yes, America has been, since the beginning of the nineteenth century, the stumbling block of tyrany, the good samaritan to the poor and unfortunate of the civilized portions of the earth, her unexampled progress the astonishment and admiration of every lover of liberty and friend of humanity, the framers of her institutions are honored as the noblest statesmen of any age, for their patriotism, purity and wisdom. And yet, strange as it may seem, this model government, this land of the free and home of the brave, presenting an aggregate of individual and national wealth, happiness and prosperity unequalled by the same numbers on the face of the earth, although in the first century of its gigantic infancy, it is now trembling with all the convulsive symptoms of revolution and civil commotion, which threatens to undermine the very basis of our institutions and our liberties. Nay, the threatening storm is now producing a tumultuous sensation that is rocking the temple of liberty from top to bottom, and from center to circumference.

Such being the sad picture of the true condition of our country, we will proceed to make earnest enquiry as to the cause of the existing evils and from whence they come; for it is a well known principle in politics, as well as every other science, that in order to apply the rightful remedy for an existing evil, it is of the utmost importance that the nature and source of the evil should be carefully studied, and thoroughly understood by those having the case in charge.

Although the threatening aspect of our national affairs have called forth the opinions of some of our most able statesmen, relative to the causes of our present troubles, yet, with due deference to their talents, sagacity and wisdom, we feel constrained to say, that, in our opinion, they have entirely overlooked, or omitted to mention, one of the chief causes that have rendered the people of the Southern States so turbulant, defiant, and, at last, nearly ungovernable.

We will now proceed to give a brief statement of what we

believe to be the source from whence most, if not all, our present difficulties can be traced, and by so doing we trust the means for restoring peace to the country will be more easily and unanimously decided upon.

In searching the political history of our country, it appears that in 1819 and '20, Congress objected to the further extension of slavery; (which, of course, it had a perfect right to do,) consequently Missouri was rejected when she applied for admission, because of her constitution recognizing that institution. At this the South became very indignant, and her statesmen predicted a speeded dissolution of the Union, unless Missouri was admitted. The result was a compromise in which the South obtained all she demanded, and then we learn nothing of her revolting spirit until the celebrated tariff difficulty came up, which called out General Jackson's proclamation, in 1832; and although that old hero stood his ground firmly and did his whole duty nobly, yet there were those who were fearful that South Carolina would injure herself, like the spoiled boy, who throws himself on the floor, and in the midst of his rage, proceeds to bruise his head against articles of a more substantial character, consequently there was a compromise effected to appease her wrath. Again, when we were about appropriating money to pay Mexico for territory obtained from her, David Wilmot offered a proviso, that inasmuch as slavery did not exist in that territory at the time it came into our possession, it should not exist there thereafter. A very wise proviso, and a vast majority of the people of the country were in favor of it, but then it did not suit the South, consequently, her statesmen predicted an immediate dissolution of the Union, if Mr. Wilmot's proviso should become a law, and, of course, most of us loved the Union, hence we threw Mr. Wilmot's proviso overboard. But shortly after that, California made application to come into the Union as a free State. This was very obnoxious to our Southern brethren, consequently, they would dissolve the Union, unless there was some concessions made. Every body was at a loss to know what the nature of the concession could be, for the government had already signed several blanks for the South to fill out to their own liking, and it was supposed, that in their wisdom, they had secured, at least, what belonged to them; but then the country was declared to be in imminent danger of a speedy dissolution, unless there could be a compromise effected with the South. All hands were set at work to ascertain whether there was anything which the government had not already granted them, and after diligent search it was found that there was occasionally a fugitive slave escaping from southern bondage, and as the people in some portions of the country were not much inclined to extend any great amount of sympathy to those who were wont to pursue said fugitives, the South finally concluded to make this proposition: That in case the government would compel every northern man to aid in catching and returning the fugitive slaves at his own cost and expense, then they, the South, would allow California to be admitted as a free State, and suffer the Union to remain undivided. Most of us remember well when this ultimatum was presented to us. We generally disliked the idea of being called blood hounds and negro catchers, by the civilized nations of the earth, saying nothing about the expense or our feelings attending this unpleasant operation, but then we loved our country, and could not think of its destruction without feelings of sadness, and when the fire-eating gentry would show their teeth, brandish their bowie knives and draw their revolvers, expressing their readiness, willingness, and final determination to shoot down, cut and carve, and smash things generally, provided we did not consent to catch Sambo; life being sweet to us, and peace being desirable, we finally concluded to save our country, even if we were compelled to chase Sambo to do it. And here again we compromised upon the basis of what was called the Fugitive Slave Law of 1850. We do not claim any great show of bravery or firmness in this case, but then if self degradation and humiliation to save our country is a mark of patriotism, we would be sorry to hear of a more patriotic people than we of the north proved ourselves to be in this transaction.

Peace being again declared to exist, things seemed to move quietly along until the winters of 1853-'54, when, to everybody's surprise, (I mean in the North,) one Stephen A. Douglas, desiring to become President of the United States, set himself at work to find out whether there was not something more which the South might have granted her to enhance her interests. Stephen, being a man of great industry and perseverance, searched carefully and thoroughly, and at last he found a restriction on the extension of the institution of slavery north of thirty-six degrees and thirty minutes north latitude. With great earnestness, and a show of fairness, he entered into the task of removing this restriction. He was soon made acquainted with the fact that this restriction was but a part of a solemn compact, and that the party for whose benefit the restriction was established, had paid for it a large price, and a disinheritance at this time would be gross injustice toward the party aggrieved.

Even some of the Southern Senators labored hard to dissuade Stephen from his purpose, on this account, but then Stephen was desirous of becoming President, and not being excessively burthened with a high sense of justice, he was inexorable in his undertaking, and pressed it with vigor and energy. Southern statesmen espoused the cause with their usual unanimity, and again declared that unless the restriction was removed this Union would be dissolved. All will remember how reluctant the people of the free States were to grant this demand; but, as in former times, we loved our country, and when its very existence was threatened we were desirous of avoiding the great calamity; hence, the restriction was removed, and the famous Kansas and Nebraska Act became a law.

Although the South had thus far been successful in obtaining whatever they demanded, nevertheless, the defiant course they had pursued, the increasing frequency, and the nature of the demands, together with their refusal to be governed by a compromise, even after dictating the terms of it themselves, began to open the eyes of some of our Northern statesmen —hence, the Republican party sprang into existence in 1854 with the avowed intention of resisting through the ballot-box each and every encroachment from our Southern brethren thereafter. This was declared by the South to be very dangerous to the Union, and in 1856, when the Republicans run a candidate in the person of John C. Fremont for the Presidency, the South declared that to be a great insult to her dignity, and a just cause for a dissolution of the Union. She blustered and threatened to such an extent that they succeeded in frightening the people of some of the free States into the support of James Buchanan, which, together with her united vote, she succeeded in carrying the election, and Mr. Buchanan became President. It soon became evident that the South were not any way inclined to abandon their aggressive policy. The attempt to subjugate the people of Kansas by forcing slavery upon them, against the well known wish of three-fourths of the inhabitants, was sufficient to wake up still another class of the people of the free States, which caused large accessions to the Republican party, and a complete division of the Democratic party. Finally, the Democrats met at Charleston on the 23d day of April, 1860, to nominate candidates for President and Vice-President. Protection for slave property in the territories was demanded by the South—it was rejected—the convention split and adjourned. The South nominated a separate candidate upon the slave protection platform, and again resorted to her old tune of declaring the Union in danger; but the people had become disgusted with this kind of electioneering, and most emphatically refused to be bullied into the support of that dogma; consequently they cast their votes for Abraham Lincoln, and elected him, which is now declared by the South to be sufficient cause for dissolving the Union. But some of the more moderate of the Southerners are willing to suffer a portion of the Union to remain undivided, provided the North will consent to amend the Constitution so as to legalize slavery as a national institution. This is a very moderate request indeed ; but, fellow countrymen, *are you ready to grant it ?*

We have thus sketched a brief history of what we believe to be the true cause of the present crisis. And why is it the cause? The answer is plain to every one—the South have been in the habit of controlling the policy of the government, by argument, if they could, but by threats of violence if they failed with the first. They have been successful in so many schemes of this kind, that they began to look upon that condition of things as co-existent with our government. Now we shall not contend that our Southern brethren are any more turbulent and ungovernable than the same number of Northern men would be, if they had been similarly dealt with. Had the government of the United States, instead of compromising with the South when threats were made, pursued a straightforward course regardless of the threats, or those who made them, and in case there had been forcible resistance to the laws, called out sufficient force to suppress the rebellion, then the people of the South would have learned one important lesson in earlier times.

This would have saved both them and the government much trouble and expense, but since they have not learned this lesson before, they should learn it now; and though they may be somewhat like an overgrown, high-spirited colt, that has never been harnessed, yet, with patience, kindness and *firmness*, we trust they will still learn the lesson without very seriously injuring either themselves or others. Should this not be the case, if they are determined to resist all legal restraint, can there be any advantage in further delaying the use of force? Can any one pretend that further concession would help the case permanently? There is no use of dodging the question. (All must admit that the great cause of our present troubles is owing to an unwillingness of the South to submit to any terms except such as they may dictate.) And some of them have even gone so far as to say that even though they are allowed this privilege, they would not abandon their treasonable designs. Verily we believe that Uncle Sam has spoiled some of his boys by over indulgence. We will endeavor to show this to be the case, by showing that, where resistance to the laws has been met by force, instead of concession, the people are more law-abiding citizens, at least we hear of no threats from that source of overthrowing the government, unless certain measures are adopted. It is a noticeable fact that, during our national existence, there has never been any concession, on the part of the government of the United States, granted to any portion of the north, where there has been resistance to the laws; but the strong arm of the government has been used to put down such resistance whenever it became necessary. The great rebellion of 1785, called Shay's Rebellion, was met with force, and the leaders punished. The great Whisky Rebellion, as it is called, was suppressed with an armed force 15,000 strong in 1794. General Washington was then president, showing that he recognised the principle of suppressing insurrection by force, if necessary to do so, in order to maintain the supremacy of the law. Again, we find the United States using force to carry out the fugitive slave law in the Burns case, and, in fact, several others. The Kansas troubles were met with force, not compromise. All these cases have occurred in the north, and have been promptly met by the government, which has had a tendency to teach the people of that section of the country that, to resist the laws, is sure to incur the legal penalty. Remonstrance has been of no avail—the laws were pointed to as the guide. This was the case particularly in the Kansas troubles, when the laws of the notorious bogus legislature were being forced upon the people by the government bayonets. Mr. Buchanan was then implored to desist, and allow the people to re-construct the laws of the territory. They were told that, although the laws were oppressive, yet so long as they remained on the statute books of the territory, they were the laws of that country, and must be enforced. This has uniformly been the course of the government toward the people of the north. We do not complain of this, but simply refer to it to show that, while the people of the north have been taught to obey the laws, or suffer the penalty of their violation, the people of the south have been allowed to control the policy of the government by threats and violence, and as might have been expected, they have at last become entirely insufferable. They will no longer be satisfied with anything in reason or out of reason. They will neither be peaceable, nor allow others to live in peace. Their demands have become more frequent and of a more startling character—and why is this? It is because they have never been made sensible of the fact that the government of the United States is capable of enforcing its laws in that portion of the country as well as in any other.

How absurd it is, then, at this time, for us to offer them another compromise—it would be like adding new fuel to the fire, it might suppress the flame momentarily, but when it bursts forth again it would be with increased vigor and violence. We should not compromise in the least if we desire permanent peace, but administer the laws with firmness and justice; and although it may take the force of arms to do so, yet a rivulet of blood, spilt at this time, will prevent rivers of it in the future. Let us not entail the evil effects of failing to perform our duty upon our children, but sternly perform our whole duty, and transmit to the next generation the good old ship of State in a sound and navigable condition; and if there be mutineers who persist in her destruction let us warn them manfully of the dangers they are incurring upon themselves, and as a last resort, rather than give up the ship, let us arrest their progress by force.

Although we have given at length what we believe to be the great primary cause of our present crisis, yet there are other more immediate causes, among which is the course that the Northern press have pursued since this secession movement has assumed a more positive form. Many of the leading papers have advocated the policy of allowing such States to secede as choose to do so. And others have been loud with their demands for concession and compromise upon any basis that would satisfy the traitors and restore peace. While still another class have battled manfully for the supremacy of the laws. This division of what is taken for the public sentiment, has been a source of consolation and encouragement to the traitors, while the government of the United States has stood silent with folded arms and allowed itself to be robbed of millions of dollars worth of property without raising a hand or uttering a solitary protest against the theft. What more encouragement could those who have been engaged in this treasonable scheme have asked for or desired? They have been told by a portion of the Democratic press that they were perfectly justifiable in dissolving the Union; and by a portion of the Republican press, that although they were by no means justifiable in committing such an outrageous act, yet, if they were really in earnest, and were determined to do so or fight, then they could go ahead, for there would be no fighting to maintain a Union with such unruly neighbors. Such seems to have been the reckless and ill-timed course on the part of the press at this present juncture, that it has encouraged the traitors by, representing the friends of the Union as divided into fragments, thus removing all opposition to their reckless course. Had the press of the North presented an unbroken front in favor of the Union, and a determination to stand by it regardless of threats or even of violence, we have every reason to believe that the South would have hesitated and considered the nature of the calamity they were bringing upon themselves and their country. That the spirit of compromise heretofore exercised on the part of our government toward those who have threatened violence, is the great source of our political troubles, can hardly admit of a doubt—why should we pursue the policy still further that has brought us to the very verge of ruin? Since it is our wavering, compromising, and undecided course that has brought our country to ruin, let us proceed to adopt a more firm and decided course. Give the South all that is their right, and boldly refuse to submit to any dictation beyond our constitutional duty. This is not the time to amend constitutions nor to change public opinion, but let every man rally to the support of his country, and when peace is restored and traitors have laid down their arms and signified a willingness to submit to the laws, we will have more leisure to investigate the nature of the proposed constitutional amendments.

THE CRISIS,

AND HOW TO MEET IT.

In the government of nations there are, sometimes, crises of the most momentous importance. They either promote stability or terminate in ruin. The result depends upon the virtue and patriotism of the mass of the people, and the wisdom, prudence and unflinching firmness of their rulers and statesmen.

The United States of America are in the midst of just such a crisis at present, and nothing is more important than correct views with regard to that crisis on the part of the people. To aid in the dissemination of such views, in order to produce unity of action among all classes of the people is the object of this publication, in which we shall ignore mere partisanship and take large and patriotic and comprehensive views of the genius and principles of our government.

One of the gravest questions for the consideration of the people of this nation, and for their enlightened solution, has just arisen, that has ever been presented for an answer since the formation of our republican government. It is this: Has any State in the Union a right, under the present Constitution, peaceably to withdraw itself from that Union, for the purpose of setting up a separate, distinct, and, necessarily, conflicting nationality?

Very important is it that this question should be correctly answered in the present juncture, and that the people should

2

be fully prepared to act understandingly. Vast and immeasurable results depend upon it.

If this vital question could be answered in the affirmative, as some seem to think, then would the federal compact, by which these States are held together, be a mere rope of sand, without strength or tenacity, subject to be ruptured by the slightest discord. Such a solution of the question, if acted upon *practically*, would carry us back to the old confederation, by the articles of which these States were connected in their associated capacity previous to the adoption of the present constitution. And what was that confederation? Merely a league of States, in which each individual member of that league was at liberty to act in her sovereign capacity, without any binding restrictions. Each individual member of that confederation could levy taxes, raise revenue, make alliances, declare war, make peace, and do whatever else she chose without consultation with the rest of the members, and without being held amenable for her action, except just so far as the general law of nations held her amenable. From that confederation she could at any time withdraw or secede, without being rebellious or traitorous to the other members.

Experience proved to the satisfaction of the wise, patriotic and far seeing fathers of the republic, that such a confederation was entirely ineffectual for the accomplishment of the great purposes for which it was formed. It possessed not the concentrated power of binding and irrepealable unity to protect the common flag of a common Union. It could not, therefore, command the respect and the honor of other nations, nor promote its own stability and permanence.

Is the present Union similar to that? Can a South Carolina, or a Massachusetts, or any other disaffected State withdraw or secede at will, as she could from the Old Confederation, and set up, if she choose, an independent nationality? No such thing. The present compact and constitution grew out of the absolute necessities consequent upon the inefficiency of the old confederation. They were established solely to prevent or obviate that inefficiency, and provide a common flag and a common government capable of commanding respect. An examination of the present Constitution will show that fact. We will, therefore, present those provisions of that instrument which have a direct bearing upon the decision of this question, and then show by the record how the fathers of that Constitution understood its powers, and how that understanding has been confirmed by all the precedents in the history of the government to the present time.

The very preamble of the Constitution itself shows that it was formed for the purpose of establishing a government stronger and more efficient than the old confederation. It is in these words:

"We, the people of the United States, in order to form a more perfect union, establish justice, ensure domestic tranquility, provide for the common defence, promote the general welfare, and secure the blessings of liberty to ourselves and our posterity, do ordain and establish this Constitution for the United States of America."

Among other things, this preamble declares that the present constitution was "ordained and established" "in order to form *a union more perfect*" than existed under the provisions of the old confederation—a union that could not be dissolved at the pleasure or choice of any State or any number of States without the consent of three-fourths of the sovereign people. It conceded to a general government certain powers and rights, which were, of course, subtracted from the powers and rights of the separate State sovereignties, and these powers and rights were vested solely in the hands of a President, "a Congress of the United States," and a Supreme Court created and elected according to the provisions of that constitution. And now, to understand this matter, what were those particular powers and rights which were thus abstracted from the separate State sovereignties and vested in a general government? They are very emphatically, clearly and forcibly declared in article I, section 8, of the constitution of the United States. They are thus expressed:

"The Congress shall have power—
"1. To lay and collect taxes, duties, imposts, excises; to pay the debts, and provide for the common defence and gen-

eral welfare of the United States; but all duties, imposts, and excises shall be uniform throughout the United States;

"2. To borrow money on the credit of the United States;

"3. To regulate commerce with foreign nations, and among the several States, and with the Indian tribes;

"4. To establish an uniform rule of naturalization, and uniform laws on the subject of bankruptcies throughout the United States;

"5. To coin money, regulate the value thereof, and of foreign coin, and fix the standard of weights and measures;

"6. To provide for the punishment of counterfeiting the securities and current coin of the United States;

"7. To establish post offices and post roads;

"8. To promote the progress of science and useful arts, by securing for limited times, to authors and inventors, the exclusive right to their respective writings and discoveries;

"9. To constitute tribunals inferior to the Supreme Court; to define and punish piracies and felonies committed on the high seas, and offences against the law of nations;

"10. To declare war, grant letters of marque and reprisal, and make rules concerning captures on land and water;

"11. To raise and support armies; but no appropriations of money to that use, shall be for a longer term than two years;

"12. To provide and maintain a navy;

"13. To make rules for the government and regulation of the land and naval forces;

"14. To provide for calling forth the militia to execute the laws of the Union, suppress insurrections, and repel invasions;

"15. To provide for organizing, arming and disciplining the militia, and for governing such part of them as may be employed in the service of the United States, reserving to the States, respectively, the appointment of the officers and the authority of training the militia, according to the discipline prescribed by Congress;

"16. To exercise exclusive legislation in all cases whatsoever, over such district (not exceeding ten miles square) as may, by cession of particular States, and the acceptance of Congress, become the seat of government of the United States, and to exercise like authority over all places purchased by the consent of the legislature of the State in which the same shall be, for the erection of forts, magazines, arsenals, dock yards and other needful buildings :—And

"17. To make all laws which shall be necessary and proper for carrying into execution the foregoing powers, and all other powers vested by this constitution in the government of the United States, or in any department or officer thereof."

The powers enumerated in this section are very definite, and nothing we could say would make that fact appear more apparent. Now if these powers are conferred upon the general government by the common consent of all the States of the Union, or more especially by all the people of all the States, can any one State exercise any of those reserved powers? Most certainly not. But the framers of the constitution did not leave this to be inferred. They settled the question definitely in section ten. Here it is:

"1. No State shall enter into any treaty, alliance, or confederation; grant letters of marque and reprisal; coin money; emit bills of credit; make anything but gold and silver coin a tender in payment of debts; pass any bill of attainder, ex post facto law, or law impairing the obligation of contracts; or grant any title of nobility.

"2. No State shall, without the consent of the Congress, lay any imposts or duties on imports or exports, except what may be absolutely necessary for executing its inspection laws; and the nett produce of all duties and imposts, laid by any State on imports or exports, shall be for the use of the treasury of the United States, and all such laws shall be subject to the revision and control of the Congress. No State shall, without the consent of Congress, lay any duty of tunnage, keep troops or ships of war in time of peace, enter into any agreement or compact with another State, or with a foreign power, or engage in war, unless actually invaded, or in such imminent danger as will not admit of delay."

This section plainly and positively *prohibits* the States from doing certain things *without the consent* of Congress. They can neither contract alliances, collect revenue, coin money, nor engage in war in their capacity of States.

To guard the powers of the general government from encroachment on the part of the States, and to preserve them intact and unimpaired, the President of the United States, as the chief Executive officer of the government, takes this oath:

"I DO SOLEMNLY SWEAR (or affirm) THAT I WILL FAITHFULLY EXECUTE THE OFFICE OF PRESIDENT OF THE UNITED STATES, AND WILL, TO THE BEST OF MY ABILITY, PRESERVE, PROTECT AND DEFEND THE CONSTITUTION OF THE UNITED STATES."

We have thus far enumerated some of the *powers* delegated by the Constitution *to the* federal government in the precise language of that constitution, and have shown that the chief executive of the government is sworn to exercise those powers by enforcing the constitution, and, of course, the laws, &c., which are made under its sanction and by its authority.

This constitution was adopted by a vast majority of the people of every State in the Union—adopted too with the understanding that it was *perpetually* binding—adopted *without any proviso for withdrawal or secession* in case of dissatisfaction—adopted when it was known that, even to amend it, either two-thirds of both houses of Congress must "propose amendments, or two-thirds of all the State Legislatures unite in an application to call a convention of States for proposing amendments," and that, when such amendments were proposed, they must *"be ratified"* by "the legislatures of *three-fourths* of all the States, or by conventions in *three-fourths* thereof." This shows clearly and conclusively that our fathers considered that they were establishing a government indissoluble—a government for all time, incapable of disruption by separate State action or by the violence of local faction.

In the strong light of these facts how are we to regard the present attitude of South Carolina? As treasonable and rebellious to rightful authority, which she herself assisted to establish. She has no right whatever, under the existing compact, to withdraw herself from the Union, or to annul that compact into which she voluntarily entered, when she adopted that constitution. By that adoption she forever signed away such a right—voluntarily she sets her signature to a compact having no such proviso of choice. If she secede then—if she break, or attempt to break, that compact, she engages in a revolution, and revolution is rebellion—revolution is *treason*. Of that capital crime she, or rather her citizens, are even now guilty. What constitutes treason? The constitution defines it in Article 3, Section III:

"1. Treason against the United States shall consist only in levying war against them, or in adhering to their enemies, giving them aid and comfort. No person shall be convicted of treason unless on the testimony of two witnesses to the same overt act, or on confession in open court.

"2. The congress shall have power to declare the punishment of treason; but no attainder of treason shall work corruption of blood, or forfeiture, except during the life of the person attainted."

Now has not South Carolina "levied war?" Has she not collected armies to resist the United States? Has she not obstructed the collection of the revenue of the nation? Has she not even taken the fortifications and arsenals and confiscated the property of the United States? All these things has she done, and if this be not "levying war"—if this be not "treason"—rank "treason," I know not what is. And yet, strange as it may seem, there are men in all the States so wedded to party that they encourage and justify South Carolina in her mad secession schemes, and by so doing give "aid and comfort" to the sworn "enemies" of the United States. Did they ever think that they too are traitors, and that they are as legally deserving of a halter as the madest secession hotspur of South Carolina?

Like the old tories of the revolution, they are, however, but few in the Northern States, and their number, thanks to the intelligence of the people, is rapidly growing less. Soon will there be but one sentiment in all sane minds upon this

subject. All will see that this Union must be preserved, unbroken by rebels, and traitors be brought to condign punishment, unless we would insanely jeopardise all for which our
fathers fought and bled and died upon the battle fields of the
revolution.

To aid in creating a healthy public sentiment upon this
important subject, I will now give some of the arguments in
favor of the Union and of the present constitution, advanced
by some of the early fathers of the republic. To do this, I
shall first draw largely from certain political papers, enti
tled the "Federalist," written while the adoption of the
present constitution was pending, and addressed to the people of the State of New York, to explain the principles of
the new constitution, and to enforce the propriety and necessity of its adoption. They were the united productions of
John Jay, James Madison, and Alexander Hamilton, three
brilliant political lights.

In the first eight numbers of these papers the dangers of
foreign force and influence, and of war between the States,
and the effects of internal war in producing standing armies
unfriendly to liberty, were portrayed in a very masterly
manner. Several other papers follow from which I quote
largely, as they are just as appropriate now to show the
benefits of a stable and consolidated Union, and the evils of
disunion, as then:

"THE UTILITY OF THE UNION AS A SAFEGUARD AGAINST DO-
MESTIC FACTION AND INSURRECTIONS.

"A firm union will be of the utmost moment to the peace
and liberty of the States, as a barrier against domestic faction and insurrection.

"It is impossible to read the history of the petty republics
of Greece and Italy, without feeling sensations of horror and
disgust at the distractions with which they were continually
agitated, and at the rapid succession of revolutions, by which
they were kept perpetually vibrating between the extremes
of tyranny and anarchy. If they exhibit occasional calms,
these only serve as short-lived contrasts to the furious storms
that are to succeed. If now and then intervals of felicity

open themselves to view, we behold them with a mixture of regret arising from the reflection, that the pleasing scenes before us are soon to be overwhelmed by the tempestuous waves of sedition and party rage. If momentary rays of glory break forth from the gloom, while they dazzle us with a transient and fleeting brilliancy, they at the same time admonish us to lament that the vices of government should pervert the direction and tarnish the luster of those bright talents and exalted endowments, for which the favored soils that produced them have been so justly celebrated.

"From the disorders that disfigure the annals of those republics, the advocates of despotism have drawn arguments, not only against the forms of republican government but against the very principles of civil liberty. They have decried all free government as inconsistent with the order of society, and have indulged themselves in malicious exultation over its friends and partizans. Happily for mankind, stupendous fabrics reared on the basis of liberty, which have flourished for ages, have, in a few glorious instances, refuted their gloomy sophisms. And, I trust, America will be the broad and solid foundation of other edifices not less magnificent, which will be equally permanent monuments of their error.

"But it is not to be denied, that the portraits they have sketched of republican government, were too just copies of the originals from which they were taken. If it had been found impracticable to have devised models of a more perfect structure, the enlightened friends of liberty would have been obliged to abandon the cause of that species of government as indefensible. The science of politics, however, like most other sciences, has received great improvement. The efficacy of various principles is now well understood, which were either not known at all, or imperfectly known to the ancients. The regular distribution of power into distinct departments; the introduction of legislative balances and checks; the institution of courts composed of judges, holding their offices during good behavior; the representation of the people in the legislature, by deputies of their own election; these are either wholly new discoveries, or have made their principal progress towards perfection in modern times. They are means, and powerful means, by which the excellencies of republican government may be retained, and its imperfections lessoned or avoided. To this catalogue of circumstances, that tend to the amelioration of popular systems of civil government, I shall venture, however novel it may appear to some, to add one more, on a principle which has been made the foundation of an objection to the new constitution; I mean the ENLARGEMENT of the ORBIT within which such systems are to revolve, either in respect to the dimensions of a single State, or to the consolidation of several smaller States into one great confederacy. The latter is that which immediately concerns the object under consideration. It will, however, be of use to examine the principle in its application to a single State, which shall be attended to in another place.

"The utility of a confederacy, as well to suppress faction, and to guard the internal tranquility of States, as to increase their external force and security, is in reality not a new idea. It has been practiced upon in different countries and ages, and has received the sanction of the most approved writers on the subject of politics. The opponents of the PLAN proposed have with great assiduity cited and circulated the observations of Montesquieu on the necessity of a contracted territory for a republican government. But they seem not to have been apprized of the sentiments of that great man expressed in another part of his work, nor to have adverted to the consequences of the principle to which they subscribe with such ready acquiescence.

When Montesquieu recommends a small extent for republics, the standards he had in view were of dimensions far short of the limits of almost every one of these States. Neither Virginia, Massachusetts, Pennsylvania, New York, N. Carolina, nor Georgia, can by any means be compared with the models from which he reasoned, and to which the terms of his description apply. If we therefore receive his ideas on this point, as the criterion of truth, we shall be driven to the alternative either of taking refuge at once in the arms of monarchy, or of splitting ourselves into an infinity of little, jealous, clashing, tumultuous commonwealths, the wretched nurseries of unceasing discord, and the miserable objects of universal pity or contempt. Some of the writers who have come forward on the other side of the question, seem to have been aware of the dilemma, and have even been bold enough to hint at the division of the larger States as a desirable thing. Such an infatuated policy, such a desperate expedient, might, by the multiplication of petty offices, answer the views of men who possess not qualifications to extend their influence beyond the narrow circles of personal intrigue; but it could never promote the greatness or happiness of the people of America.

"Referring the examination of the principle itself to an other place, as has been already mentioned, it will be sufficient to remark here, that in the sense of the author who has been most emphatically quoted upon the occasion, it would only dictate a reduction of the SIZE of the more considerable MEMBERS of the Union; but would not militate against their being all comprehended in one confederate government. And this is the true question, in the discussion of which we are at present interested.

"So far are the suggestions of Montesquieu from standing in opposition to a general union of the States, that he explicitly treats of a CONFEDERATE REPUBLIC, as the expedient for extending the sphere of popular government, and reconciling the advantages of monarchy with those of republicanism.

" 'It is very probable, says he, *that mankind would have been obliged, at length, to live constantly under the government of a SINGLE PERSON, had they not contrived a kind of constitution, that has all the internal advantages of a republican, together with the external force of a monarchical government. I mean a CONFEDERATE REPUBLIC.

" 'This form of government is a convention, by which several smaller *States* agree to become members of a larger *one*, which they intend to form. It is a kind of assemblage of societies, that constitute a new one, capable of increasing by means of new associations, till they arrive to such a degree

*Spirit of Laws, Vol. I, Book IX, Chapter I.

of power as to be able to provide for the security of the united body.

"'A republic of this kind, able to withstand an external force, may support itself without any internal corruption. The form of this society prevents all manner of inconveniences.

"'If a single member should attempt to usurp the supreme authority, he could not be supposed to have an equal authority and credit in all the confederate States. Were he to have too great influence over one, this would alarm the rest. Were he to subdue a part, that which would still remain free might oppose him with forces, independent of those which he had usurped, and overpower him before he could be settled in his usurpation.

"'Should a popular insurrection happen in one of the confederate States, the others are able to quell it. Should abuses creep into one part, they are reformed by those that remain sound. The State may be destroyed on one side and not on the other; the confederacy may be dissolved and the confederates preserve their sovereignty.

"'As this government is composed of small republics, it enjoys the internal happiness of each, and with respect to its external situation, it is possessed, by means of the association, of all the advantages of large monarchies.'

"I have thought it proper to quote at length these interesting passages, because they contain a luminous abridgment of the principal arguments in favor of the Union, and must effectually remove the false impressions which a misapplication of the other parts of the work were calculated to produce. They have, at the same time, an intimate connection with the more immediate design of this paper; which is to illustrate the tendency of the Union to repress domestic faction and insurrection.

"A distinction, more subtle than accurate, has been raised between a *confederacy* and a *consolidation* of the States. The essential characteristic of the first, is said to be the restriction of its authority to the members in their collective capacities, without reaching to the individuals of whom they are composed. It is contended that the national council ought to have no concern with any object of internal administration. An exact equality of suffrage between the members, has also been insisted upon as a leading feature of a confederate government. These positions are, in the main, arbitrary; they are supported neither by principle nor precedent. It has indeed happened, that governments of this kind have generally operated in the manner which the distinction taken notice of supposes to be inherent in their nature; but there have been in most of them extensive exceptions to the practice, which serve to prove, as far as example will go, that there is no absolute rule on the subject. And it will be clearly shown, in the course of this investigation, that, as far as the principle contended for has prevailed, it has been the cause of incurable disorder and imbecility in the government.

"The definition of a *confederate republic* seems simply to be 'an assemblage of societies,' or an association of two or more States into one State. The extent, modifications, and objects of the federal authority are mere matters of discretion. So long as the separate organization of the members be not abolished, so long as it exists by a constitutional necessity for local purposes, though it should be in perfect subordination to the general authority of the Union, it would still be, in fact and theory, an association of States, or a confederacy. The proposed constitution, so far from implying an abolition of the State government, makes them constituent parts of the national sovereignty, by allowing them a direct representation in the senate, and leaves in their possession certain exclusive, and very important, portions of the sovereign power. This fully corresponds, in every rational import of the terms, with the idea of a federal government.

"In the Lycian confederacy, which consisted of twenty-three CITIES, or republics, the largest were entitled to *three* votes in the COMMON COUNCIL, those of the middle class to *two*, and the smallest to *one*. The COMMON COUNCIL had the appointment of all the judges and magistrates of the respective CITIES. This was certainly the most delicate species of interference in their internal administration; for if there be anything that seems exclusively appropriated to the local jurisdictions, it is the appointment of their own officers. Yet

Montesquieu, speaking of this association, says, 'Were I to give a model of an excellent confederate republic, it would be that of Lycia.' Thus we perceive that the distinctions insisted upon were not within the contemplation of this enlightened writer, and we shall be led to conclude that they are the novel refinements of an erroneous theory."

The important paper just quoted from the "Federalist," is from the gifted pen of James Madison, so long a prominent and leading statesman in the democratic party, and one of the framers of our present government. Had we space we would quote another, equally important, from the same source and upon the same subject.

This paper, its pointed facts and its powerful reasoning in favor of a stable Union, such as was contemplated by the present constitution, and against the defects of the old confederation, we commend to the particular attention of the thinking masses of the present democratic party. Although written before the adoption of the existing constitution, and for the express purpose of inducing the people to ratify that constitution, it contains much that is applicable to the present political juncture, inasmuch as the present secession dogmas of South Carolina and of the Calhoun school of politicians are exactly the loose, inefficient principles of that old confederation, and opposed to those of the present constitution.

We will here make an extract from another paper of the "Federalist," to show how Jay, Madison and Hamilton regarded the defects of that confederation—to illustrate, with clearness, the *absolute necessity* of the adoption of our present constitution, considering, as they did, that it would constitute an efficient remedy for those defects :

"CONCERNING THE DEFECTS OF THE PRESENT CONFEDERATION, IN RELATION TO THE PRINCIPLE OF LEGISLATION FOR THE STATES IN THEIR COLLECTIVE CAPACITIES.

"In the course of the preceding papers, I have endeavored, my fellow citizens, to place before you, in a clear and convincing light, the importance of union to your political safety and happiness. I have unfolded to you a complication of dangers to which you would be exposed, should you permit that sacred knot, which binds the people of America together, to be severed or dissolved by ambition or by avarice, by jealousy or by misrepresentation. In the sequel of the inquiry, through which I propose to accompany you, the truths intended to be inculcated will receive further confirmation from facts and arguments hitherto unnoticed.

"In pursuance of the plan which I have laid down for the discussion of the subject, the point next in order to be examined is the 'insufficiency of the present confederation to the preservation of the Union.'

"It may perhaps be asked what need there is of reasoning or proof to illustrate a position which is neither controverted nor doubted; to which the understandings and feelings of all classes of men assent; and which, in substance is admitted by the opponents as well as by the friends of the new constitution? It must in truth be acknowledged, that however these may differ in other respects, they in general appear to harmonize in the opinion, that there are material imperfections in our national system, and that something is necessary to be done to rescue us from impending anarchy. The facts that support this opinion are no longer objects of speculation. They have forced themselves upon the sensibility of the people at large, and have at length extorted from those whose mistaken policy has had the principal share in precipitating the extremity at which we have arrived, a reluctant confession of the reality of many of those defects in the scheme of our federal government, which have been long pointed out and regretted by the intelligent friends of the Union.

"We may indeed with propriety, be said to have reached almost the last stage of national humiliation. There is scarcely anything that can wound the pride, or degrade the character, of an independent people, which we do not experience. Are there engagements, to the performance of which we are held by every tie respectable among men? These are the subjects of constant and unblushing violation. Do we owe debts to foreigners, and to our own citizens, contracted in a time of imminent peril, for the preservation of our political existence? These remain without any proper or satisfactory provision for their discharge. Have we valuable territories and important posts in the possession of a foreign power, which, by express stipulations, ought long since to have been surrendered? These are still retained, to the prejudice of our interest not less than of our rights. Are we in a condition to resent or to repel the aggression? We have neither troops, nor treasury, nor government.* Are we even in a condition to remonstrate with dignity? The just imputations on our own faith, in respect to the same treaty, ought first to be removed. Are we entitled, by nature and compact, to a free participation in the navigation of the Mississippi? Spain excludes us from it. Is public credit an indispensable resource in time of public danger? We seem to have abandoned its cause as desperate and irretrievable. Is commerce of importance to national wealth? Ours is at the lowest point of declension. Is respectability in the eyes of foreign powers, a safeguard against foreign encroachments? The imbecility of our government even forbids them to treat with us: Our ambassadors abroad are the mere pageants of mimic sovereignty. Is a violent and unnatural decrease in the value of land a symptom of national distress? The price of improved land, in most parts of the country, is much lower than can be accounted for by the quantity of waste land at market, and can be only fully explained by that want of private and public confidence, which are so alarmingly prevalent among all ranks, and which have a direct tendency to depreciate property of every kind. Is private credit the friend and patron of industry? That most useful kind which relates to borrowing and lending, is reduced within the narrowest limits, and this still more from an opinion of insecurity than from a scarcity of money. To shorten an enumeration of particulars which can afford neither pleasure nor instruction, it may in general be demanded, what indication is there of national disorder, poverty, and insignificance, that could befal a community so peculiarly blessed with

---

* I mean for the Union.

natural advantages as we are, which does not form a part of the dark catalogue of our public misfortunes?

"This is the melancholy situation to which we have been brought by those very maxims and councils, which would now deter us from adopting the proposed constitution; and which, not content with having conducted us to the brink of a precipice, seem resolved to plunge us into the abyss that awaits us below. Here, my countrymen, impelled by every motive that ought to influence an enlightened people, let us make firm stand for our safety, our tranquility, our dignity, our reputation. Let us at last break the fatal charm which has too long seduced us from the paths of felicity and prosperity.

"It is true, as has been before observed, that facts too stubborn to be resisted, have produced a species of general assent to the abstract proposition, that there exist material defects in our national system; but the usefulness of the concession, on the part of the old adversaries of federal measures, is destroyed by a strenuous opposition to a remedy, upon the only principles that can give it a chance of success. While they admit that the government of the United States is destitute of energy, they contend against conferring upon it those powers which are requisite to supply that energy. They seem still to aim at things repugnant and irreconcilable; at an augmentation of federal authority, without a diminution of State authority; at sovereignty in the Union, and complete independence in the members. They still, in fine, seem to cherish with blind devotion the political monster of an *imperium in imperio*. This renders a full display of the principal defects of the confederation necessary, in order to show, that the evils we experience do not proceed from minute or partial imperfections, but from fundamental errors in the structure of the building, which cannot be amended, otherwise than by an alteration in the very elements and main pillars of the fabric.

"The great and radical vice in the construction of the existing confederation, is in the principle of LEGISLATION for STATES or GOVERNMENTS in their CORPORATE or COLLECTIVE CAPACITIES, and as contradistinguished from the INDIVIDUALS

3

of whom they consist. Though this principle does not run through all the powers delegated to the Union, yet it pervades and governs those on which the efficacy of the rest depends."

A violation of any of the articles of the old confederation was the act only of the States, as sovereign and independent parties to a contract, and did not implicate individuals in the crime of *treason*, if acting *under the sanction* of such a State. Not so, however, with individuals under the present constitution, even though acting under the sanction of particular States; because the present constitution is that of the *people* and not of the States as States in their sovereign capacity, for the *people* of the States have delegated to a general government, in the constitution, certain powers, which are taken away from the States, and cannot, therefore, be exercised by those States without subjecting the *people* of the States so exercising them to punishment for *high treason*.

To show that eminent statesmen, even before the adoption of our present constitution, so regarded the principles of the government proposed to be established under it, we will quote another extract from the "Federalist," commencing on page 102 of vol. I:

"If it be possible to construct a federal government capable of regulating the common concerns, and preserving the general tranquility, it must be founded, as to the objects committed to its care, upon the REVERSE of the principle contended for by the opponents of the proposed constitution. It must carry its agency to the PERSONS OF THE CITIZENS. It must stand in need of no intermediate legislation; but must itself be empowered to employ the arm of the ordinary magistrate to execute its own resolutions. The majesty of the national authority must be manifested through the medium of the courts of justice. The government of the Union, like that of each State, must be able to address itself immediately to the hopes and fears of INDIVIDUALS, and to attract to its support those passions which have the strongest influence upon the human heart. It must, in short, possess all the means, and have a right to all the methods, of excuting tho powers with which it is entrusted, that are possessed and exercised by the governments of the particular States."

An argument against the adoption of our present constitution was urged by its enemies to prevent its adoption, that it would create a central government *too strong*—a government *so strong* as to endanger the reserved rights of the States. This objection is thus stated and answered upon pages 106 and 107, vol. I, of the "Federalist:"

"It may be said, that it would tend to render the government of the Union too powerful, and to enable it to absorb those residuary authorities which it might be judged proper to leave with the States for local purposes. Allowing the utmost latitude to the love of power, which any reasonable man can require, I confess I am at a loss to discover what temptation the persons entrusted with the administration of the general government, could ever feel to divest the States of the authorities of that description. The regulation of the mere domestic police of a State appears to me to hold out slender allurements to ambition. Commerce, finance, negotiation, and war seem to comprehend all the objects which have charms for minds governed by that passion; and all the powers necessary to those objects ought, in the first instance, to be lodged in the national depository. The administration of private justice between the citizens of the same State; the supervision of agriculture, and of other concerns of a similar nature; all those things, in short, which are proper to be provided for by local legislation, can never be desirable cares of a general jurisdiction. It is, therefore, improbable that there should exist a disposition in the federal councils to usurp the powers with which they are connected; because the attempt to exercise them would be as troublesome as it would be nugatory; and the possession of them, for that reason, would contribute nothing to the dignity, to the importance, or to the splendor of the national government."

We will close our extracts from the luminous papers of the "Federalist," with the following, premising, however, that, in these fearful times of raging secession madness, it would be well if the whole two volumes could be put in the hands of every intelligent individual in the nation. This extract refers again to the defects and the lamentable inefficiency of the old confederation, as contrasted with the proposed efficiency and stability of the government under the new constitution, a subject which cannot be too deeply engraven upon the mind of every patriot to whatever party he may belong. It can be found commencing upon page 131, of vol. 1, of the "Federalist," and ending on page 133:

"Having in the three last numbers taken a summary review of the principal circumstances and events which depict the genius and fate of other confederate governments, I shall now proceed in the enumeration of the most important of those defects which have hitherto disappointed our hopes from the system established among ourselves. To form a safe and satisfactory judgment of the proper remedy, it is absolutely necessary that we should be well acquainted with the extent and malignity of the disease.

"The next most palpable defect of the existing confederation, is the total want of a SANCTION to its laws. The United States, as now composed, have no power to exact obedience, or punish disobedience to their resolutions, either by pecuniary mulets, by a suspension or divestiture of privileges, or by any other constitutional means. There is no express delegation of authority to them to use force against delinquent members; and if such a right should be ascribed to the federal head, as resulting from the nature of the social compact between the States, it must be by inference and construction, in the face of that part of the second article, by which it is declared, 'that each State shall retain every power, jurisdiction, and right, not *expressly* delegated to the United States in Congress assembled.' The want of such a right involves, no doubt, a striking absurdity, but we are reduced to the dilemma, either of supposing that deficiency, preposterous as it may seem, or of contravening or explaining away a provision, which has been of late a repeated theme of the eulogies of those who oppose the new constitution; and the omission of which, in that plan, has been the subject of much plausible animadversion and severe criticism. If we are unwilling to impair the force of this applauded provision, we shall be obliged to conclude that the United States affords the extraordinary spectacle of a government destitute even of the shadow of constitutional power to enforce the execution of its own laws. It will appear, from the specimens which have been cited, that the American confederacy, in this particular, stands discriminated from every other institution of a similar kind, and exhibits a new and unexampled phenomenon in the political world.

"The want of a mutual guarantee of the State governments, is another capital imperfection in the federal plan. There is nothing of this kind declared in the articles that compose it; and to imply a tacit guarantee from considerations of utility, would be a still more flagrant departure from the clause which has been mentioned, than to imply a tacit power of coercion, from the like consideration. The want of a guarantee, though it might in its consequences endanger the Union, does not so immediately attack its existence, as the want of a constitutional sanction to its laws.

"Without a guarantee, the assistance to be derived from the Union in repelling those domestic dangers, which may sometimes threaten the existence of the State constitutions, must be renounced. Usurpation may rear its crest in each State, and trample upon the liberties of the people, while the national government could legally do nothing more than behold its encroachments with indignation and regret. A successful faction may erect a tyranny on the ruins of order and law, while no succor could constitutionally be afforded by the Union to the friends and supporters of the government. The tempestuous situation, from which Massachusetts has scarcely emerged, evinces, that dangers of this kind are not merely speculative. Who can determine what might have been the issue of her late convulsions, if the mal-contents had been headed by a Cæsar or by a Cromwell? Who can predict what a despotism, established in Massachusetts, would have upon the liberties of New Hampshire or Rhode Island, of Connecticut or New York?

"The inordinate pride of State importance has suggested to some minds an objection to the principle of a guarantee to the federal government, as involving an officious interference in the domestic concerns of the members. A scruple of this kind would deprive us of one of the principal advantages to be expected from Union, and can only flow from a misapprehension of the nature of the provision itself. It could be no impediment to reforms of the State constitutions by a majority of the people in a legal and peaceable mode. This right would remain undiminished. The guarantee could only operate against changes to be effected by violence. Towards the prevention of calamities of this kind, too many checks cannot be provided. The peace of society and the stability of government depend absolutely on the efficacy of the precautions on this head. Where the whole power of the government is in the hands of the people, there is the less pretence for the use of violent remedies, in partial or occasional distempers of the State. The natural cure for an ill-administration, in a popular representative constitution, is a change of men. A guarantee by the national authority would be as much directed against the usurpations of rulers, as against the ferments and outrages of faction and sedition in the community."

We have thus far briefly enumerated some of the important powers granted by the people of the United States in their sovereign capacity, to the present federal government. We have endeavored to show that the people, having granted certain powers to the general government, such powers are necessarily withdrawn from the several States by the people thereof for the purpose of establishing one grand central power, which, when exercised within its delegated authority, should be recognized as the supreme law of the land; hence the people of the several States having to the extent of the powers granted, surrendered the separate State sovereignty, they became one grand, inseparable, sovereign and independent nation. The very fact that each and every citizen of our entire country has a voice in controlling the policy of the general government, shows conclusively that they owe obedience to its enactments, consequently, our national laws are alike binding upon every individual from Florida to Maine, and from the Atlantic to the Pacific Ocean.

But independent of our arguments, we have in the foregoing pages presented copious extracts from letters written by Messrs. Madison, Jay and Hamilton pending the adoption of the constitution, all of which must convince the most skeptical, that all parties at that time understood that they were granting certain powers to the general government that could not thereafter be resumed and controlled by the various States. The able manner in which the importance of such an arrangement is argued, the clear and conclusive reasoning, the contrasts drawn between one great and powerful nation and several petty, jealous, contending little sovereignties, should cast into the shade the weak sophism that is palmed off by the political demagogues of the present day for the purpose of dividing the people, under the disguise of what is called State sovereignty.

The arguments already advanced to show that we have a national government whose authority is supreme throughout the length and breadth of this country, (State laws to the contrary notwithstanding,) should be sufficient to convince the most ultra States rights secessionist that his dogma is only a garbled name for treason. Nevertheless, we will now proceed to give in full the celebrated Proclamation issued to the nullifiers of South Carolina twenty-eight years ago by the hero of the battle of New Orleans, recommending its careful perusal by every American citizen who has a spark of patriotism left within him. Its noble, patriotic sentiments will be found decidedly refreshing when contrasted with the crouching imbecility and indecision that has characterized not only James Buchanan but many of our leading politicians in the present dangerous, suffering and distracted condition of our beloved country.

General Jackson, a brave, daring, noble hero, knowing his duty, hastened to perform it in defiance of every obstacle; he resolves to save his country, at every hazard, from falling into the vortex of anarchy, ruin and disgrace.

When the hydra-headed monster, treason, began to make

its appearance, the honored son of Tennessee, whose name is
held in reverence by every friend of liberty, whose memory
will be honored as the savior of his country, actuated by a
high sense of his duty, with true Roman firmness, standing
upon the temple of liberty, proclaiming to the world that he
will maintain the integrity of his country or perish while
marching under its glorious banner warning the enemies of
the Union, to pause and consider the awful consequences
of persisting in their treasonable designs, and decide whether they are prepared to assume such a terrible responsibility.

I will now give his proclamation in full, hoping that the
spirit of patriotism, firmness and justice therein contained
will cause a heartfelt response by my fellow countrymen.

PRESIDENT'S PROCLAMATION.

Proclamation of Andrew Jackson, President of the United States.

WHEREAS, A convention assembled in the State of South Carolina have passed an ordinance, by which they declare "That the several acts and parts of acts of the congress of the United States, purporting to be laws for the imposing of duties and imposts on the importation of foreign commodities, and now having actual operation and effect within the United States, and more especially," two acts for the same purposes passed on the 29th of May, 1828, and on the 14th of July, 1832, "are unauthorized by the constitution of the United States, and violate the true meaning and intent thereof, and are null and void, and no law," nor binding on the citizens of that State or its officers: and by the said ordinance, it is further declared to be unlawful for any of the constituted authorities of the State or of the United States to enforce the payment of the duties imposed by the said acts within the same State, and that it is the duty of the Legislature to pass such laws as may be necessary to give full effect to the said ordinance:

AND WHEREAS, By the said ordinance, it is further ordained that, in no case of law or equity decided in the courts of said State, wherein shall be drawn in question the validity of the said ordinance, or of the acts of the legislature that may be passed to give it effect, or of the said laws of the United States, no appeal shall be allowed to the Supreme Court of the United States, nor shall any copy of the record be permitted or allowed for that purpose, and that any person attempting to take such appeal shall be punished as for a contempt of court:

And, finally, the said ordinance declares that the people of South Carolina will maintain the said ordinance at every hazard; and that they will consider the passage of any act, by congress, abolishing or closing the ports of the said State, or otherwise obstructing the free ingress or egress of vessels to and from the said ports, or any other act of the Federal Government to coerce the State, shut up her ports, destroy or harrass her commerce, or to enforce the said acts otherwise than through the civil tribunals of the country, as inconsistant with the longer continuance of South Carolina in the Union, and that the people of the said State will thenceforth hold themselves absolved from all further obligation to maintain or preserve their political connection with the people of the other States, and will forthwith proceed to organize a separate government, and do all other acts and things which sovereign and independent States may of right do.

AND WHEREAS, the said ordinance prescribes to the people of South Carolina a course of conduct in direct violation of their duty as citizens of the United States, contrary to the laws of their country, subversive of its constitution, and having for its object the destruction of the Union—that Union, which, coeval with our political existence, led our fathers, without any other ties to unite them than those of patriotism and a common cause, through a sanguinary struggle to a glorious independence—that sacred Union, hitherto inviolate, which, perfected by our happy constitution, has brought us, by the favor of Heaven, to a state of prosperity at home, and high consideration abroad, rarely, if ever, equalled in the history of nations. To preserve this bond of our political existence from destruction, to maintain inviolate this state of national honor and prosperity, and to justify the confidence my fellow citizens have reposed in me, I, ANDREW JACKSON, *President of the United States*, have thought proper to issue this my PROCLAMATION, stating my views of the constitution and laws applicable to the measures adopted by the convention of South Carolina, and to the reasons they have put forth to sustain them, declaring the course which duty will require me to pursue, and, appealing to the understanding and patriotism of the people, warn them of the consequences that must inevitably result from an observance of the dictates of the convention.

Strict duty would require of me nothing more than the exercise of those powers with which I am now, or may hereafter be invested, for preserving the peace of the Union, and for the execution of the laws. But the imposing aspect which opposition has assumed in this case, by clothing itself with State authority, and the deep interest which the people of the United States must all feel in preventing a resort to stronger measures, while there is a hope that anything will be yielded to reasoning and remonstrance, perhaps demand, and will certainly justify, a full exposition to South Carolina and the nation of the views I entertain of this important question, as well as a distinct enunciation of the course which my sense of duty will require me to pursue.

The ordinance is founded, not on the indefeasible right of resisting acts which are plainly unconstitutional, and too oppressive to be endured; but on the strange position that any one State may not only declare an act of congress void, but prohibit its execution—that they may do this consistently with the constitution—that the true construction of that instrument permits a State to retain its place in the Union, and yet be bound by no other of its laws than those it may choose to consider as constitutional. It is true, they add, that to justify this abrogation of a law, it must be palpably contrary to the constitution; but it is evident, that, to give the right of resisting laws of that description, coupled with the uncontrolled right to decide what laws deserve that character, is to give the power of resisting all laws. For, as by the theory, there is no appeal, the reasons alleged by the State, good or bad must prevail. If it should be said that public opinion is a sufficient check against the abuse of this power, it may be asked why it is not deemed a sufficient guard against the passage of an unconstitutional act by congress? There is, however, a restraint in this last case, which makes the assumed power of a State more indefensible, and which does not exist in the other. There are two appeals from an unconstitutional act passed by congress—one to the judiciary, the other to the people and the States. There is no appeal from the State decision in theory, and the practical illustration shows that the courts are closed against an application to review it, both judges and jurors being sworn to decide in its favor. But reasoning on this subject is superfluous, when our social compact, in express terms, declares that the laws of the United States, its constitution, and treaties made under it, are the supreme law of the land; and, for greater caution, adds "that the judges in every State shall be bound thereby, anything in the constitution or laws of any State to the contrary notwithstanding." And it may be asserted without fear of refutation, that no federal government could exist without a similar provision. Look for a moment to the consequence. If South Carolina considers the revenue laws unconstitutional, and has a right to prevent their execution in the port of Charleston, there would be a clear constitutional objection to their collection in every other port, and no revenue could be collected anywhere; for all imposts must be equal. It is no answer to repeat, that an unconstitutional law is no law, so long as the question of its legality is to be decided by the State itself; for every law operating injuriously upon any local interest will be perhaps thought, and certainly represented, as unconstitutional, and, as has been shown, there is no appeal.

If this doctrine had been established at an earlier day, the Union would have been dissolved in its infancy. The excise law in Pennsylvania, the embargo and non-intercourse law in the eastern States, the carriage tax in Virginia, were all deemed unconstitutional, and were more equal in their operation than any of the laws now complained of; but fortunately none of those States discovered that they had the right now claimed by South Carolina. The war into which we were forced to support the dignity of the nation and the rights of our citizens, might have ended in defeat and disgrace instead of victory and honor, if the States who supposed it a ruinous and unconstitutional measure, had thought they possessed the right of nullifying the act by which it was declared, and denying supplies for its prosecution. Hardly and unequally as those measures bore upon several members of the Union, to the legislatures of none did this efficient and peaceable remedy, as it is called, suggest itself. The discovery of this important feature in our constitution was reserved to the present day. To the statesmen of South Carolina belongs the invention, and upon the citizens of that State will unfortunately fall the evils of reducing it to practice.

If the doctrine of a State veto upon the laws of the Union carries with it internal evidence of its impracticable absurdity, our constitutional history will also afford abundant proof that it would have been repudiated with indignation, had it been proposed to form a feature in our Government.

In our colonial state, although dependent on another power, we very early considered ourselves as connected by common interest with each other. Leagues were formed for common defence, and, before the declaration of independence, we were known in our aggregate character *as the United Colonies of America.* That decisive and important step was taken jointly. We declared ourselves a nation by a joint, not by several acts, and when the terms of our confederation were reduced to form, it was in that of a solemn league of several States, by which they agreed that they would collectively form one nation for the purpose of conducting some certain domestic concerns and all foreign relations. In the instrument forming that Union is found an article which declares that "every State shall abide by the determinations of congress on all questions which, by that confederation, should be submitted to them."

Under the confederation, then, no State could legally annul a decision of the congress, or refuse to submit to its execution; but no provision was made to enforce these decisions. Congress made requisitions, but they were not complied with. The government could not operate on individuals. They had no judiciary, no means of collecting revenue.

But the defects of the confederation need not be detailed. Under its operation we could scarcely be called a nation. We had neither prosperity at home nor consideration abroad. This state of things could not be endured, and our present happy constitution was formed, but formed in vain, if this fatal doctrine prevails. It was formed for important objects that are announced in the preamble made in the name and by the authority of the people of the United States, whose delegates framed, and whose conventions approved it. The most important among these objects, that which is placed first in the rank, on which all others rest, is, *"to form a more perfect Union."* Now, is it possible that even if there were no express provision giving supremacy to the constitution and laws of the United States over those of the States—can it be conceived, that an instrument made for the purpose of *"forming a more perfect Union"* than that of the confederation, could be so constructed by the assembled wisdom of our country as to substitute for that confederation a form of government dependent for its existence on the local interest, the party spirit of a State, or of a prevailing faction in a State? Every man of plain, unsophisticated understanding, who hears the question, will give such an answer as will preserve the Union. Metaphysical subtlety, in pursuit of an impracticable theory, could alone have devised one that is calculated to destroy it.

I consider, then, the power to annul a law of the United States, assumed by one State, *incompatible with the existence of the Union, contradicted expressly by the letter of the constitution, unauthorized by its spirit, inconsistent with every principle on which it was founded, and destructive of the great object for which it was formed.*

After this general view of the leading principle, we must examine the particular application of it which is made in the ordinance.

The preamble rests its justification on these grounds: It assumes, as a fact, that the obnoxious laws, although they purport to be laws for raising revenue, were in reality intended for the protection of manufactures, which purpose it asserts to be unconstitutional; that the operation of these laws is unequal; that the amount raised by them is greater than is required by the wants of the government; and, finally, that the proceeds are to be applied to objects unauthorized by the constitution. These are the only causes alleged to justify an open opposition to the laws of the country, and a threat of seceding from the Union, if any attempt should be made to enforce them. The first virtually acknowledges that the law in question was passed under a power expressly given by the constitution to lay and collect imposts;

but its constitutionality is drawn in question from the *motives* of those who passed it. However apparent this purpose may be in the present case, nothing can be more dangerous than to admit the position that an unconstitutional purpose, entertained by the members who assent to a law enacted under a constitutional power, shall make the law void : for how is that purpose to be ascertained? Who is to make the scrutiny? How often may bad purposes be falsely imputed—in how many cases are they concealed by false professions—in how many is no declaration of motive made? Admit this doctrine, and you give to the States an uncontrolled right to decide, and every law may be annulled under this pretext. If, therefore, the absurd and dangerous doctrine should be admitted, that a State may annul an unconstitutional law, or one that it deems such, it will not apply to the present case.

The next objection is, that the laws in question operate unequally. This objection may be made with truth to every law that has been or can be passed. The wisdom of man never yet contrived a system of taxation that would operate with perfect equality. If the unequal operation of a law makes its unconstitutional, and if all laws of that description may be abrogated by any State for that cause, then indeed is the Federal Constitution unworthy of the slightest effort for its preservation. We have hitherto relied on it as the perpetual bond of our Union. We have received it as the work of the assembled wisdom of the nation. We have trusted to it as to the sheet anchor of our safety in the stormy times of conflict with a foreign or domestic foe. We have looked to it with sacred awe as the palladium of our liberties, and with all the solemnities of religion have pledged to each other our lives and fortunes here, and our hopes of happiness hereafter, in its defence and support. Were we mistaken, my countrymen, in attaching this importance to the Constitution of our country? Was our devotion paid to the wretched, inefficient, clumsy, contrivance which this new doctrine would make it? Did we pledge ourselves to the support of an airy nothing—a bubble that must be blown away by the first breath of disaffection? Was this self-destroying, visionary theory, the work of the profound statesmen, the exalted patriots, to whom the task of constitutional reform was entrusted? Did the name of Washington sanction, did the States deliberately ratify such an anomaly in the history of fundamental legislation? No. We were not mistaken. The letter of this great instrument is free from this radical fault; its language directly contradicts the imputation; its spirit—its evident intent, contradicts it. No, we did not err! Our Constitution does not contain the absurdity of giving power to make laws, and another power to resist them. The sages whose memory will always be reverenced, have given us a practical, and, as they hoped, a permanent constitutional compact. The Father of his Country did not affix his revered name to so palpable an absurdity. Nor did the States, when they severally ratified it, do so under the impression that a veto on the laws of the United States was reserved to them, or that they could exercise it by implication. Search the debates in all their Conventions, examine the speeches of the most zealous opposers of federal authority, look at the amendments that were proposed—they are all silent—not a syllable uttered, not a vote given, not a motion made, to correct the explicit supremacy given to the laws of the Union over those of the States, or to show that implication, as is now contended, could defeat it. No, we have not erred! The Constitution is still the object of our reverence, the bond of our Union, our defence in danger, the source of our prosperity in peace; it shall descend as we have received it, uncorrupted by sophistical construction, to our posterity, and the sacrifices of local interest, of State prejudices, of personal animosities, that were made to bring it into existence, will again be patriotically offered for its support.

The two remaining objections made by the ordinance to these laws, are that the sums intended to be raised by them are greater than are required, and that the proceeds will be unconstitutionally employed.

The Constitution has given, expressly, to Congress the right of raising revenue, and of determining the sum the public exigencies will require. The States have no control over the exercise of this right other than that which results from the power of changing the representatives who abuse it, and thus procure redress. Congress may, undoubtedly, abuse this discretionary power; but the same may be said of others with which they are vested. Yet the discretion must exist somewhere. The Constitution has given it to the representatives of all the people, checked by the representatives of the States, and by the Executive power. The South Carolina construction gives it to the Legislature or the Convention of a single State, where neither the people of the different States, nor the States in their separate capacity, nor the Chief Magistrate elected by the people, have any representation. Which is the most discreet disposition of the power? I do not ask you, fellow citizens, which is the constitutional disposition—that instrument speaks a language not to be misunderstood. But if you were assembled in general Convention, which would you think the safest depository of this discretionary power in the last resort? Would you add a clause giving it to each of the States, or would you sanction the wise provisions already made by your Constitution? It this should be the result of your deliberations when providing for the future, are you, can you be ready, to risk all that we hold dear, to establish, for a temporary and a local purpose, that which you must acknowledge to be destructive, and even absurd, as a general provision? Carry out the consequences of this right vested in the different States, and you must perceive that the crisis your conduct presents at this day would recur whenever any law of the United States displeased any of the States, and that we should soon cease to be a nation.

The ordinance, with the same knowledge of the future that characterizes a former objection, tells you that the proceeds of the tax will be unconstitutionally applied. If this could be ascertained with certainty, the objection would, with more propriety, be reserved for the law so applying the proceeds, but surely cannot be urged against the laws levying the duty.

These are the allegations contained in the ordinance. Examine them seriously, my fellow-citizens; judge for yourselves. I appeal to you to determine whether they are so clear, so convincing, as to leave no doubt of their correctness; and even if you should come to this conclusion, how far they justify the reckless, destructive course which you are directed

4

to pursue. Review these objections, and the conclusions
drawn from them, once more. What are they? Every law,
then, for raising revenue, according to the South Carolina
ordinance, may be rightfully annulled, unless it be so framed
as no law ever will or can be framed. Congress have a right
to pass laws for raising a revenue, and each State has a right
to oppose their execution—two rights directly opposed to
each other; and yet is this absurdity supposed to be contained
in an instrument drawn for the express purpose of avoiding
collisions between the States and the general government, by
an assembly of the most enlightened statesmen and purest
patriots ever embodied for a similar purpose.

In vain have these sages declared that congress shall have
power to lay and collect taxes, duties, imposts, and excises;
in vain have they provided that they shall have power to
pass laws, which shall be necessary and proper to carry those
powers into execution ; that those laws and that constitution
shall be the "supreme law of the land, and that the judges
in every State shall be bound thereby, anything in the constitution or laws of any State to the contrary notwithstanding." In vain have the people of the several States solemnly
sanctioned these provisions, made them their paramount law,
and individually sworn to support them whenever they were
called on to execute any office. Vain provisions! ineffectual
restrictions! vile profanation of oaths! miserable mockery
of legislation! if the bare majority of the voters in any one
State may, on a real or supposed knowledge of the intent
with which a law has been passed, declare themselves free
from its operation—say here it gives too little, there too
much, and operates unequally—here it suffers articles to be
free that ought to be taxed—there it taxes those that ought
to be free—in this case the proceeds are intended to be applied
to purposes which we do not approve—in that the amount
raised is more than is wanted. Congress, it is true, are invested by the constitution with the right of deciding these
questions according to their sound discretion ; congress is
composed of the representatives of all the States, and of all
the people of all the States ; but we, part of the people of
one State, to whom the constitution has given no power on
the subject, from whom it has expressly taken it away—we,

who have solemnly agreed that this constitution shall be our law—we, most of whom have sworn to support it—we now abrogate this law, and swear and force others to swear that it shall not be obeyed; and we do this, not because congress have no right to pass such laws—this we do not allege—but because they have passed them with improper views. They are unconstitutional from the motives of those who passed them, which we can never with certainty know; from their unequal operation, although it is impossible, from the nature of things, that they should be equal; and from the disposition which we presume may be made of their proceeds, although that disposition has not been declared. This is the plain meaning of the ordinance, in relation to laws which it abrogates for alleged unconstitutionality. But it does not stop there. It repeals, in express terms, an important part of the constitution itself, and of laws passed to give it effect, which have never been alleged to be unconstitutional. The constitution declares that the judicial powers of the United States extend to cases arising under the laws of the United States; and that such laws, the constitution, and treaties, shall be paramount to the State constitutions and laws. The judiciary act prescribes the mode by which the case may be brought before a court of the United States by appeal, when a State tribunal shall decide against this provision of the constitution. The ordinance declares that there shall be no appeal, makes the State law paramount to the constitution and laws of the United States, forces judges and jurors to swear that they will disregard their provisions, and even makes it penal in a suitor to attempt relief by appeal. It further declares, that it shall not be lawful for the authorities of the United States, or of that State, to enforce the payment of duties imposed by the revenue laws within its limits.

Here is a law of the United States, not even pretended to be unconstitutional, repealed by the authority of a small majority of the voters of a single State. Here is a provision of the constitution, which is solemnly abrogated by the same authority.

On such expositions and reasonings, the ordinance grounds not only an assertion of the right to annul the laws, of which

it complains, but to enforce it by a threat of seceding from
the Union, if any attempt is made to execute them.

This right to secede is deduced from the nature of the constitution, which they say is a compact between sovereign
States, who have preserved their whole sovereignty, and
therefore are subject to no superior; that because they made
the compact, they can break it, when, in their opinion, it has
been departed from by the other States. Fallacious as this
course of reasoning is, it enlists State pride, and finds advocates in the honest prejudices of those, who have not studied
the nature of our government sufficiently to see the radical
error, on which it rests.

The people of the United States formed the constitution,
acting through the State legislatures in making the compact,
to meet and discuss its provisions, and acting in separate conventions, when they ratified those provisions; but the terms
used in its construction, show it to be a government, in which
the people of all the States collectively are represented. We
are *one people* in the choice of president and vice president.
Here the States have no other agency, than to direct the
mode in which the votes shall be given. The candidates
having a majority of all the votes are chosen. The electors
of a majority of States may have given their votes for one
candidate, and yet another may be chosen. The people, then,
and not the States, are represented in the executive branch.

In the house of representatives there is this difference, that
the people of one State do not, as in the case of president and
vice president, all vote for the same officers. The people of
all the States do not vote for all the members, each State electing only its own representatives. But this creates no material distinction. When chosen, they are all representatives
of the United States, not representatives of the particular
State from whence they come. They are paid by the United
States, not by the State; nor are they accountable to it for
any act done in the performance of their legislative functions; and however they may in practice, as it is their duty
to do, consult and prefer the interests of their particular
constituents, when they come in conflict with any other partial or local interest, yet it is their first and highest duty, as

a representative of the United States, to promote the general good.

The constitution of the United States, then, forms a *government*, not a league; and whether it be formed by compact between the States, or in any other manner, its character is the same. It is a government, in which all the people are represented, which operates directly on the people individually, not upon the States; they retained all the power they did not grant. But each State having expressly parted with so many powers, as to constitute jointly with the other States a single nation, cannot from that period possess any right to secede, because such secession does not break a league, but destroys the unity of a nation; and any injury to that unity is not only a breach, which would result from the contravention of a compact, but it is an offence against the whole Union. To say that any State may at pleasure secede from the Union, is to say that the United States are not a nation; because it would be a solecism to contend, that any part of a nation might dissolve its connection with the other parts, to their injury or ruin, without committing any offence. Secession, like any other revolutionary act, may be morally justified by the extremity of oppression; but to call it a constitutional right, is confounding the meaning of terms; and can only be done through gross error, or to deceive those, who are willing to assert a right, but would pause before they made a revolution, or incur the penalties consequent on a failure.

Because the Union was formed by compact, it is said the parties to that compact may, when they feel themselves aggrieved, depart from it; but it is precisely because it is a compact, that they cannot. A compact is an agreement, or binding obligation. It may, by its terms, have a sanction or penalty for its breach, or it may not. If it contains no sanction, it may be broken with no other consequence than moral guilt; if it have a sanction, then the breach incurs the designated or implied penalty. A league between independent nations generally has no sanction, other than a moral one; or, if it should contain a penalty, as there is no common superior, it cannot be enforced. A government, on the contrary, always has a saction, express or implied; and in our case, it is both necessarily implied, and expressly given. An attempt by force of arms to destroy a government, is an offence, by whatever means the constitutional compact may have been formed; and such government has the right, by the law of self-defence, to pass acts for punishing the offender, unless that right is modified, restrained, or resumed by the constitutional act. In our system, although it is modified in the case of treason, yet authority is expressly given to pass all laws necessary to carry its powers into effect, and under this grant provision has been made for punishing acts, which obstruct the due administration of the laws.

It would seem superfluous to add anything to show the nature of that Union, which connects us; but as erroneous opinions on this subject are the foundation of doctrines the most destructive to our peace, I must give some further development to my views on this subject. No one, fellow-citizens, has a higher reverence for the reserved rights of the States, than the magistrate, who now addresses you. No one would make greater personal sacrifices, or official exertions to defend them from violation; but equal care must be taken to prevent, on their part, an improper interference with, or resumption of the rights they have vested in the nation. The line has not been so distinctly drawn, as to avoid doubts in some cases of the exercise of power. Men of the best intentions, and soundest views, may differ in their construction of some parts of the constitution; but there are others, on which dispassionate reflection can leave no doubt. Of this nature appears to be the assumed right of secession. It rests, as we have seen, on the alleged undivided sovereignty of the States, and on their having formed, in this sovereign capacity, a compact, which is called the constitution, from which, because they made it, they have the right to secede. Both of these positions are erroneous, and some of the arguments to prove them so have been anticipated.

The States severally have not retained their entire sovereignty. It has been shown, that, in becoming parts of a nation, not members of a league, they surrendered many of their essential parts of sovereignty. The right to make treaties, declare war, levy taxes, exercise exclusive judicial and legislative powers, were all of them functions of sovereign power. The States, then, for all these purposes, were no longer sovereign. The allegiance of their citizens was transferred, in the first instance, to the government of the United States; they became American citizens, and owed obedience to the constitution of the United States, and to laws made in conformity with the powers it vested in congress. This last position has not been, and cannot be denied. How, then, can that State be said to be sovereign and independent whose citizens owe obedience to laws not made by it, and whose magistrates are sworn to disregard those laws when they come in conflict with those passed by another? What shows conclusively that the States cannot be said to have reserved an undivided sovereignty, is, that they expressly ceded the right to punish treason, not treason against their separate power, but treason against the United States. Treason is an offence against *sovereignty*, and sovereignty must reside with the power to punish it. But the reserved rights of the States are not less sacred because they have, for their common interest, made the general government the depository of these powers.

The unity of our political character (as has been shown for another purpose) commenced with its very existence. Under the royal government we had no separate character: our opposition to its oppressions began as *united colonies*. We were the *United States* under the confederation, and the name was perpetuated, and the Union rendered more perfect by the federal constitution. In none of these stages did we consider ourselves in any other light than as forming one nation. Treaties and alliances were made in the name of all. Troops were raised for the joint defence. How, then, with all these proofs, that under all changes of our position we had, for designated purposes and with defined powers, created national governments; how is it, that the most perfect of those several modes of union should now be considered as a mere league, that may be dissolved at pleasure? It is from an abuse of terms. "Compact" is used as synonymous with "league," although the true term is not employed, because it would at once show the fallacy of the reasoning. It would not do to say, that our constitution was only a league; but it is labored to prove it a compact, (which in one sense it is,) and then to argue, that, as a league is a compact, every compact between nations must of course be a league, and that from such an engagement every sovereign power has a right to recede. But it has been shown, that in this sense the States are not sovereign, and that even if they were, and the national constitution had been formed by compact, there would be no right in any one State to exonerate itself from its obligations.

So obvious are the reasons, which forbid this secession, that it is necessary only to allude to them. The Union was formed for the benefit of all. It was produced by mutual sacrifices of interests and opinions. Can those sacrifices be recalled? Can the States, who magnanimously surrendered their title to the territories of the west, recall the grant? Will the inhabitants of the inland States agree to pay the duties, that may be imposed without their assent, by those on the Atlantic or the Gulf, for their own benefit? Shall there be a free port in one State, and onerous duties in another? No one believes, that any right exists, in a single State, to involve the others in these and countless other evils, contrary to the engagements solemnly made. Every one must see, that the other States, in self-defence, must oppose it at all hazards.

These are the alternatives, that are presented by the convention: A repeal of all the acts for raising revenue, leaving the government without the means of support; or an acquiescence in the dissolution of our Union by the secession of one of its members. When the first was proposed, it was known, that it could not be listened to for a moment. It was known, if force was applied to oppose the execution of the laws, that it must be repelled by force; that congress could not, without involving itself in disgrace, and the country in ruin, accede to the proposition; and yet, if this is not done on a given day, or if any attempt is made to execute the laws, the State is, by the ordinance, declared to be out of the Union. The majority of a convention assembled for the purpose have dictated these terms, or rather this rejection of all terms, in the name of the people of South Carolina. It is true, that the governor of the State speaks of the submission of their grievances to a convention of all the States, which, he says, they "sincerely and anxiously seek and desire." Yet this obvious and constitutional mode of obtaining the sense of the other States, on the construction of the federal compact, and amending it if necessary, has never been attempted by those, who have urged the State on to this destructive measure. The State might have proposed the call for a general convention to the other States; and congress, if a sufficient number of them concurred, must have called it. But the first magistrate of South Carolina, when he expressed a hope, that, "on a review by congress and the functionaries of the general government of the merits of the controversy," such a convention will be accorded to them, must have known, that neither congress, nor any functionary of the general government, has authority to call such a convention, unless it be demanded by two-thirds of the States. This suggestion, then, is another instance of the reckless inattention to the provisions of the constitution, with which this crisis has been madly hurried on; or of the attempt to persuade the people, that a constitutional remedy had been sought and refused. If the legislature of South Carolina "anxiously desire" a general convention to consider their complaints, why have they not made application for it, in the way the constitution points out? The assertion, that they "earnestly seek" it, is completely negatived by the omission.

This, then, is the position in which we stand. A small majority of the citizens of one State in the Union have elected delegates to a State Convention; that Convention has ordained that all the revenue laws of the United States must be repealed, or that they are no longer a member of this Union. The Governor of that State has recommended to the Legislature the raising of an army to carry the secession into effect, and that he may be empowered to give clearances to vessels in the name of the State. No act of violent opposition to the laws has yet been committed, but such a state of things is hourly apprehended; and it is the intent of this instrument to proclaim, not only that the duty imposed on me by the Constitution "to take care that the laws be faithfully executed," shall be performed to the extent of the powers already vested in me by law, or of such others as the wisdom of Congress shall devise and entrust to me for that purpose, but to warn the citizens of South Carolina who have been deluded into an opposition to the laws, of the danger they will incur by obedience to the illegal and disorganizing ordinance of the Convention; to exhort those who have refused to support it to persevere in their determination to uphold the Constitution and laws of their country; and to point out to all the perilous situation into which the good people of that State have been led, and that the course they are urged to pursue is one of ruin and disgrace to the very State whose rights they affect to support.

Fellow citizens of my native State, let me not only admonish you, as the First Magistrate of our common country, not to incur the penalty of its laws, but use the influence that a father would over his children whom he saw rushing to certain ruin. In that paternal language, with that paternal feeling, let me tell you, my countrymen, that you are deluded by men who are either deceived themselves, or wish to deceive you. Mark under what pretences you have been led on to the brink of insurrection and treason, on which you stand! First, a diminution of the value of your staple commodity, lowered by over production in other quarters, and the consequent diminution in the value of your lands, were the sole effect of the tariff laws.

The effect of those laws was confessedly injurious, but the evil was greatly exaggerated by the unfounded theory you were taught to believe, that its burthens were in proportion to your exports, not to your consumption of imported articles. Your pride was roused by the assertion that a submission to those laws was a state of vassalage, and that resistance to them was equal, in patriotic merit, to the opposition our fathers offered to the oppressive laws of Great Britain. You were told that this opposition might be peaceably—might be constitutionally made; that you might enjoy all the advantages of the Union, and bear none of its burthens. Eloquent appeals to your passions, to your State pride, to

your native courage, to your sense of real injury, were used
to prepare you for the period when the mask, which concealed the hideous features of disunion, should be taken off. It
fell, and you were made to look with complacency on objects
which, not long since, you would have regarded with horror.
Look back to the arts which have brought you to this state
—look forward to the consequences to which it must inevitably lead! Look back to what was first told you as an induce-
ment to enter into this dangerous course. The great political truth was repeated to you, that you had the revolutionary right of resisting all laws that were palpably unconstitutional and intolerably oppressive; it was added that the
right to nullify a law rested on the same principle, but that
it was a peaceable remedy! This character which was given
to it, made you receive, with too much confidence, the asser-
tions that were made of the unconstitutionality of the law
and its oppressive effects. Mark, my fellow citizens, that, by
the admission of your leaders, the unconstitutionality must
be *palpable*, or it will not justify either resistance or nullification! What is the meaning of the word *palpable*, in the
sense in which it is here used? that which is apparent to every
one; that which no man of ordinary intellect will fail to perceive. Is the unconstitutionality of these laws of that description? Let those among your leaders who once approved
and advocated the principle of protective duties, answer the
question; and let them choose whether they will be considered as incapable, then, of perceiving that which must have
been apparent to every man of common understanding, or
as imposing upon your confidence, and endeavoring to mis-
lead you now. In either case, they are unsafe guides in the
perilous path they urge you to tread. Ponder well on this
circumstance, and you will know how to appreciate the exaggerated language they address to you. They are not cham-
pions of liberty emulating the fame of our revolutionary fathers; nor are you an oppressed people, contending, as they
repeat to you, against worse than colonial vassalage.

  You are free members of a flourishing and happy Union.
There is no settled design to oppress you. You have indeed
felt the unequal operation of laws which may have been un-

wisely, not unconstitutionally passed; but that inequality must necessily be removed. At the very moment when you were madly urged on to the unfortunate course you have begun, a change in public opinion had commenced. The nearly approaching payment of the public debt, and the consequent necessity of a diminution of duties, had already produced a considerable reduction, and that, too, on some articles of general consumption in your State. The importance of this change was underrated, and you were authoritatively told that no further alleviation of your burthens were to be expected at the very time when the condition of the country imperiously demanded such a modification of the duties as should reduce them to a just and equitable scale. But, as if apprehensive of the effect of this change in allaying your discontents, you were precipitated into the tearful state in which you now find yourselves.

I have urged you to look back to the means that were used to hurry you on to the position you have now assumed, and forward to the consequences it will produce. Something more is necessary. Contemplate the condition of that country of which you still form an important part. Consider its government uniting in one bond of common interest and general protection so many different States—giving to all their inhabitants the proud title of American citizens, protecting their commerce, securing their literature and their arts; facilitating their intercommunication; defending their frontiers; and making their name respected in the remotest parts of the earth. Consider the extent of its territory; its increasing and happy population; its advance in arts, which render life agreeable; and the sciences, which elevate the mind! See education spreading the lights of religion, morality, and general information into every cottage in this wide extent of our Territories and States? Behold it as the asylum where the wretched and the oppressed find a refuge and support! Look on this picture of happiness and honor, and say—*we, too, are citizens of America!* Carolina is one of these proud States—her arms have defended—her best blood has cemented this happy Union! And then add, if you can, without horror and remorse, this happy Union we will dissolve; this picture of peace and prosperity we will deface; this free intercourse we will interrupt; these fertile fields we will deluge with blood; the protection of that glorious flag we renounce; the very name of Americans we discard. And for what, mistaken men—for what do you throw away these inestimable blessings? for what would you exchange your share in the advantages and honor of the Union? For the dream of separate independence—a dream interrupted by bloody conflicts with your neighbors, and a vile dependence on a foreign power. If your leaders could succeed in establishing a separation, what would be your situation? Are you united at home —are you free from the apprehension of civil discord, with all its fearful consequences? Do our neighboring republics, every day suffering some new revolution, or contending with some new insurrection—do they excite your envy? But the dictates of a high duty obliges me solemnly to announce that you cannot succeed. The laws of the United States must be executed. I have no discretionary power on the subject—my duty is emphatically pronounced in the Constitution. Those who told you that you might peaceably prevent their execution, deceived you—they could not have been deceived themselves. They know that a forcible opposition could alone prevent the execution of the laws, and they know that such opposition must be repelled. Their object is disunion; but be not deceived by names; disunion, by armed force, is *treason*. Are you really ready to incur its guilt? If you are, on the heads of the instigators of the act be the dreadful consequences—on their heads be the dishonor. but on yours may fall the punishment; on your unhappy State will inevitably fall all the evils of the conflict you force upon the government of your country. It cannot accede to the mad project of disunion, of which you would be the first victims—its First Magistrate cannot, if he would, avoid the performance of his duty; the consequences must be fearful for you, distressing to your fellow citizens here, and to the friends of good government throughout the world. Its enemies have beheld our prosperity with a vexation they could not conceal—it was a standing refutation of their slavish doctrines, and they will point to our discord with the triumph of malignant joy. It is yet in your power to disappoint them. There is yet time to show that the descendants of the Pinckneys, the Sumters, the Rutledges, and of the thousand other names which adorn the pages of your revolutionary history, will not abandon that Union, to support which so many of them fought, and bled, and died.

I adjure you, as you honor their memory—as you love the cause of freedom, to which they dedicated their lives—as you prize the peace of your country, the lives of its best citizens, and your own fair fame, to retrace your steps. Snatch from the archives of your State the disorganizing edict of its Convention—bid its members to re-assemble, and promulgate the decided expressions of your will to remain in the path which alone can conduct you to safety, prosperity, and honor. Tell them that, compared to disunion, all other evils are light, because that brings with it an accumulation of all. Declare that you will never take the field unless the star spangled banner of your country shall float over you; that you will not be stigmatized when dead, and dishonored and scorned while you live, as the authors of the first attack on the Constitution of your country. Its destroyers you cannot be. You may disturb its peace—you may interrupt the course of its prosperity—you may cloud its reputation for stability, but its tranquility will be restored, its prosperity will return, and the stain upon its national character will be transferred, and remain an eternal blot on the memory of those who caused the disorder.

Fellow citizens of the United States! The threat of unhallowed disunion—the names of those once respected, by whom it is uttered—the array of military force to support it—denote the approach of a crisis in our affairs, on which the continuance of our unexampled prosperity, our political existence, and perhaps that of all free governments, may depend. The conjuncture demanded a free, a full, and explicit enunciation, not only of my intentions, but of my principles of action; and as the claim was asserted of a right by a State to annul the laws of the Union, and even to secede from it at pleasure, a frank exposition of my opinions in relation to the origin and form of our government, and the construction I give to the instrument by which it was created, seemed to be proper. Having the fullest confidence in the justness of the legal and constitutional opinion of my duties, which has been expressed, I rely, with equal confidence, on your undivided support in my determination to execute the laws—to preserve the Union by all constitutional means—to arrest, if possible, by moderate but firm measures, the necessity of a recourse to force; and, if it be the will of Heaven, that the recurrence of its primeval curse on man for the shedding of a brother's blood should fall upon our land, that it be not called down by any offensive act on the part of the United States.

Fellow-citizens! the momentous case is before you. On your undivided support of your government depends the decision of the great question it involves, whether your sacred Union will be preserved, and the blessings it secures to us as one people, shall be perpetuated. No one can doubt that the unanimity with which that decision will be expressed, will be such as to inspire new confidence in republican institutions, and that the prudence, the wisdom, and the courage which it will bring to their defence, will transmit them unimpaired and invigorated to our children.

May the great Ruler of Nations grant that the signal blessings with which he has favored ours, may not, by the madness of party or personal ambition, be disregarded and lost; and may His wise providence bring those who have produced this crisis to see their folly, before they feel the misery of civil strife, and inspire a returning veneration for that Union, which, if we may dare to penetrate his designs, he has chosen as the only means of attaining the high destinies to which we may reasonably aspire.

In testimony whereof, I have caused the seal of the United States to be hereunto affixed, having signed the same with my hand.

Done at the city of Washington, this 10th day of December, in the year of our Lord one thousand eight hundred and thirty-two, and of the independence of the United States the fifty-seventh.   ANDREW JACKSON.

By the President:
    EDW. LIVINGSTON, *Secretary of State.*

Comment upon the imperishable document just quoted is entirely unnecessary. It speaks for itself in thundering tones that strikes terror to the traitor's heart. Mark the clear and lucid reasoning,* the kind, paternal advice, the bold and manly warning that pervades this production, of the true, noble, honored patriot of the Hermitage.

For the purpose of contrasting the administration of Andrew Jackson, during the convulsion of 1832–'33, with that of James Buchanan, during our present similar condition, we will give a brief summary of the course pursued by the former:

On the 24th day of November, previous to the issuing of President Jackson's proclamation, South Carolina had, through her convention, effectually declared herself out of the Union, by an ordinance that was to take effect on the first day of February, 1833. The President, being apprehensive of trouble in collecting the duties imposed by congress in the various ports of South Carolina, and more especially at Charleston, dispatched, through his secretary of the treasury, Louis McLean, confidential orders of the most strict and positive character, to the collectors at the several ports of entry.

He writes to James K. Prinkle, Esq., collector at Charleston, ordering him to use the utmost firmness and vigilence in seeing the laws promptly executed in every particular. He

---

*Joseph Story, LL. D., although a most bitter political opponent of Gen. Jackson, in his commentaries on the constitution of the United States, thus refers to the proclamation:

"While this sheet was passing through the press, President Jackson's proclamation of the 10th of December, 1832, concerning the recent ordinance of South Carolina on the subject of the tariff, appeared. That document contains a most elaborate view of several questions, which have been discussed in this and the preceding volume, especially respecting the supremacy of the laws of the Union; the right of the judiciary to decide upon the constitutionality of those laws; and the total repugnancy to the constitution of the modern doctrine of nullification asserted in that ordinance. As a State paper it is entitled to very high praise for the clearness, force and eloquence, with which it has defended the rights and powers of the national government. I gladly copy into these pages some of its important passages, as among the ablest commentaries ever offered upon the constitution."

ordered the revenue cutter Alert to proceed to Charleston, and, in writing to Mr. Prinkle, he says, you will, moreover, cause the officers of the cutter (showing that there were others at hand), under your direction, to board all vessels departing from the port of Charleston, and in case any shall be found without having been regularly entered and cleared in the manner required by law, to seize and detain the same, to be prosecuted according to law. The number of assistants and employees were greatly increased, and every precaution taken to prevent a surprise. But as time rolled around South Carolina, not having penetrated the purposes of President Jackson sufficiently to understand his position, felt confident in her final success, and was defiant in her attitude. She began to collect her army that was to defeat the government of the United States. She had appealed to her sister States to aid her in sustaining her position. Dissatisfaction had already began to show itself in various other sections of the country. The President beheld the dangers and felt the responsibility resting upon him, and on the 10th day of December he issued his Proclamation, declaring his unalterable purpose to enforce the laws and collect the duties, and above all to stand by the Constitution and the Union to the last, and warning those who were precipitating their country into a civil war to beware of the consequences and fearful responsibility they would incur by a continuance in their reckless course.

But South Carolina had gone too far to be silenced by any ordinary means. She continued her preparations, still hoping that she could spread disaffection into other portions of the country sufficient to frighten the government into granting her demands, and many of the true friends of the Union trembled for its safety, so wide-spread was the sympathy South Carolina had enlisted. Many members of Congress were ready with their measures of pacification, each anxious to become the instrument of settling the difficulty, and perhaps immortalize his name. The horrors of civil war were as freely discussed as at the present day. Numerous were those who were ready and willing to sacrifice everything, even the dignity of the nation, to avert the dreadful calamity. But where was the brave Jackson? He was at the helm of the

5

great ship of State, and although the storm was raging, and the billows threatening to engulf her or dash her to fragments on the inhospitable shore of anarchy, yet the brave old hero, with the Constitution for his guide and the God of liberty for his counselor, bid defiance to the mutineers who were threateningly assembled around him.

On the 16th day of December he sent a special message to Congress asking for additional legislation for the purpose of meeting the exigency, he reminding them of their sworn duty to protect the Constitution from every encroachment, and appealed to their patriotism, and urged them, as true Americans, to stand firmly by their country. Congress promptly responded to the call, and the President thus prepared continued the collection of customs uninterruptedly, and preserved the honor and dignity of the nation.

South Carolina, after much blustering and threatening, quieted down, and it is to be hoped that many of the leaders of the rebellion lived to see the folly of their acts and the wisdom of the President.

But let us look for a moment at the course James Buchanan has pursued. It is now over a year since men occupying high places in the government began to publicly avow their determination to destroy this government and involve all in one common ruin. Public speeches and the press of the country have all proclaimed the determination of certain partain parties to break up this Union. Conventions have been held and resolutions passed declaring certain States out of the Union. Arsenals have been seized, forts have been taken by bodies of armed men, public property confiscated, and an unarmed steamer, bearing the flag of the nation, has been fired into for attempting to comply with government orders —collectors of customs are arrested and tried for treason for performing their duty. The free navigation of the Mississippi is prevented; American citizens are driven out of several of the States while peaceably attending to their legitimate business, and some of the more unfortunate have suffered tarring and feathering, whipping, scourging and even death at the hands of those acting under authority, or at least within the knowledge of the authorities of the several

States; and yet, after all the enumerated outrages, sufficient to disgrace even the half-civilized nation of Morocco, not one word of unqualified rebuke has James Buchanan uttered against those committing these outrages, not only against our government but the very name of humanity. Surrounded by treason in his own cabinet,* he has looked quietly on while his Secretary of War supplied the insurgents with government arms. Open and defiant traitors have been his daily counselors, while his imbecile, undecided course gives no one confidence in his future policy. Treason is now openly and boldly perpetrated throughout at least one-third of the entire country without the least restraint from any source whatever.

If there is to be found within the pages of history where the government of a great, powerful and prosperous nation suffered treason to spread over one-third of the entire country, coupled with the open and revolting acts of violence that have characterized this rebellion, without the first attempt to check its destructive progress, it is not within the range of my knowledge.

Although the grounds for argument to show that this government was established by the people collectively of the whole country, (and not by the several States, as claimed by some,) and that it can only be rightfully altered or abolished by a constitutional majority of the same power that established it, would seem to have been entirely gone over, nevertheless we propose to introduce the additional evidence of that noble, honored statesman, and able constitutional expounder, Daniel Webster.

On the 21st day of January, 1830, Mr. Hayne delivered in the Senate of the United States a very able speech advocating the right of the various States to nullify the laws of Congress in certain contingencies, or what might be more properly called the South Carolina doctrine, embracing the right to nullify the laws of Congress, or declare herself out of the Union at pleasure. His speech was considered a complete

---

* We are happy to say that within a few days he has dismissed some, and others, disgusted with their own acts, have withdrawn.

success by the advocates of his sentiments, and was thought by them an unanswerable vindication of those principles, and when Mr. Webster undertook the task of replying to Mr. Hayne, he was met with jeers by the friends of nullication; but as the volume of his reasoning began to unfold itself, all eyes were attentively turned toward the speaker. After proceeding to state the grounds upon which was founded the pretended right to nullify the acts of Congress, Mr. Webster said :

"This leads us to inquire into the origin of this government and the source of its power. Whose agent is it? Is it the creature of the State legislatures, or the creature of the people? If the government of the United States be the agent of the State governments, then they may control it, provided they can agree in the manner of controlling it; if it is the agent of the people, then the people alone can control it, restrain it, modify or reform it. It is observable enough, that the doctrine for which the honorable gentleman contends leads him to the necessity of maintaining, not only that this general government is the creature of the States, but that it is the creature of each of the States severally; so that each may assert the power, for itself, of determining whether it acts within the limits of its authority. It is the servant of four and twenty masters, of different wills and purposes; and yet bound to obey all. This absurdity (for it seems no less) arises from a misconception as to the origin of this government, and its true character. It is, sir, the people's constitution, the people's government; made for the people; made by the people; and answerable to the people. The people of the United States have declared that this constitution shall be the supreme law. We must either admit the proposition, or dispute their authority. The States are unquestionably sovereign, so far as their sovereignty is not affected by this supreme law. The State legislatures, as political bodies, however sovereign, are yet not sovereign over the people. So far as the people have given power to the general government, so far the grant is unquestionably good, and the government holds of the people, and not of the State governments. We are all agents of the same supreme power, the people. The general government and the State governments derive their authority from the same source. Neither can, in relation to the other, be called primary; though one is definite and restricted, and the other general and residuary.

"The national government possesses those powers which it can be shown the people have conferred on it, and no more. All the rest belongs to the State governments, or to the people themselves. So far as the people have restrained State sovereignty by the expression of their will, in the constitution of the United States, so far, it must be admitted, State sovereignty is effectually controlled. I do not contend that it is, or ought to be, controlled further. The sentiment to which I have referred propounds that State sovereignty is only to be controlled by its own 'feelings of justice;' that is to say, it is not to be controlled at all; for one who is to follow his feelings, is under no legal control. Now, however men may think this ought to be, the fact is, that the people of the United States have chosen to impose control on State sovereignties. The constitution has ordered the matter differently from what this opinion announces. To make war, for instance, is an exercise of sovereignty; but the constitution declares that no State shall make war. To coin money is another exercise of sovereign power; but no State is at liberty to coin money. Again, the constitution says, that no sovereign State shall be so sovereign as to make a treaty. These prohibitions, it must be confessed, are a control on the State sovereignty of South Carolina, as well as of the other States, which does not arise 'from feelings of honorable justice.' Such an opinion, therefore, is in defiance of the plainest provisions of the constitution."

Mr. Webster proceeded to investigate the South Carolina doctrine as it was then termed; he referred to the resolutions of Pennsylvania and Kentucky declaring the tariff laws constitutional, while in South Carolina the same laws were declared to be a palpable, deliberate usurpation of power by Congress; and in speaking of the absurdity of allowing each State to decide in such cases, he said:

"If there be no power to settle such questions, independent of either of the States, is not the whole Union a rope of sand? Are we not thrown back again precisely upon the old confederation?

"It is too plain to be argued. Four and twenty interpreters of constitutional law, each with a power to decide for itself, and none with authority to bind anybody else, and this constitutional law the only bond of their union! What is such a state of things but a mere connection during pleasure, or, to use the praseology of the times, *during feeling?* And that feeling, too, not the feeling of the people who established the constitution, but the feeling of the State governments."

In referring to remarks made by Mr. Hayne, concerning what Mr. Hillhouse should have said about not being bound to obey an unconstitutional law, Mr. Webster says:

"He quotes that distinguished senator as saying, that in his judgment the embargo law was unconstitutional, and that, therefore, in his opinion, the people were not bound to obey it.

"That, sir, is perfectly constitutional language. As unconstitutional law is not binding; *but then it does not rest with a resolution or a law of a State legislature to decide whether an act of congress be or be not constitutional.* An unconstitutional act of congress would not bind the people of this District although they have no legislature to interfere in their behalf; and, on the other hand, a constitutional law of congress does bind the citizens of every State, although all their legislatures should undertake to annul it, by act or resolution. The venerable Connecticut senator is a constitutional lawyer, of sound principles and enlarged knowledge; a statesman practiced and experienced, bred in the company of Washington, and holding just views upon the nature of our governments. He believed the embargo unconstitutional, and so did others; but what then? Who did he suppose was to decide that question? The State legislature? Certainly not. No such sentiment ever escaped his lips."

Mr. Webster went on to ask from whence this supposed right of the States came? Where did they get the power to interfere with the laws of the Union? He contended that the notion was founded in a misapprehension of the origin of this government and of the foundation on which it stands. I hold, said he, this to be a popular government, erected by the people, those who administer it responsible to the people, and itself capable of being amended and modified just as the people may choose it should be.

"It is as popular, just as truly emenating from the people, as the State governments. It is created for one purpose; the State governments for another. It has its own powers; they have theirs. There is no more authority with them to arrest the operation of a law of congress, than with congress to arrest the operation of their laws. We are here to administer a constitution emenating immediately from the people, and trusted by them to our administration. It is not the creature of the State governments. It is of no moment to the argument that certain acts of the State legislatures are necessary to fill our seats in this body. That is not one of their original State powers, a part of the sovereignty of the State. It is a duty which the people, by the constitution itself, have imposed on the State legislatures, and which they might have left to be performed elsewhere, if they had seen fit. So they have left the choice of president with electors; but all this does not affect the proposition that this whole government—president, senate and house of representatives—is a popular government. It leaves it still all its popular character. The governor of a State (in some of the States) is chosen not directly by the people for the purpose of performing, among other duties, that of electing a governor. Is the government of the State on that account not a popular government? This government, sir, is the independent offspring of the popular will. It is not the creature of State legislatures; nay, more, if the whole truth must be told, the people brought it into existence, established it, and have hitherto supported it, for the very purpose, amongst others, of imposing certain salutary restraints on State sovereignties.

The States cannot now make war; they cannot contract alliances; they cannot make, each for itself, separate regulations of commerce; they cannot lay imposts; they cannot coin money. If this constitution, sir, be the creature of State legislatures, it must be admitted that it has obtained a strange control over the volition of its creators."

Mr. Webster then proceeded to show that when the people erected this government they gave it a Constitution, and in that Constitution they enumerated the powers which they bestowed on it. That they had made it a limited government, and defined its authority and restrained it to the exercise of such powers as were granted, and all others were reserved to the States or the people. But they did not stop there, being aware that no Constitution could be so plainly written but what there would be a difference of opinion on the construction of some points, consequently they (the people) in order to avoid a recurrence of the difficulties experienced under the old confederacy and render the laws of Congress effective and binding upon all parties without applying to State authority, thus rendering the government complete within itself, declared the Constitution and the laws of the United States, made in pursuance thereof, should be the supreme law of the land. In referring to the tribunal in which to decide questions arising under the Constitution, Mr Webster said :

" But, sir, the people have wisely provided, in the constitution itself, a proper, suitable mode and tribunal for settling questions of constitutional law. There are, in the constitution, grants of powers to congress, and restrictions on those powers. There are also prohibitions on the States. Some authority must therefore necessarily exist, having the ultimate jurisdiction to fix and ascertain the interpretation of these grants, restrictions, and prohibitions. The constitution has itself pointed out, ordained, and established that authority. How has it accomplished this great and essential end? By declaring, sir, that '*the constitution and the laws of the United States, made in pursuance thereof, shall be the supreme law of the land, anything in the constitution or laws of any State to the contrary notwithstanding.'*

"This, sir, was the first great step. By this, the supremacy of the constitution and laws of the United States is declared. The people so will it. No State law is to be valid which comes in conflict with the constitution or any law of the United States. But who shall decide this question of interference? To whom lies the last appeal? This, sir, the constitution itself decides also, by declaring *'that the judicial power shall extend to all cases arising under the constitution and laws of the United States.'* These two provisions, sir, cover the whole ground. They are, in truth, the keystone of the arch. With these it is a government; without them it is a confederacy. In pursuance of these clear and express provisions, congress established, at its very first session, in the judicial act, a mode for carrying them into full effect, and for bringing all questions of constitutional power to the final decision of the supreme court. It then, sir, became a government. It then had the means of self-protection; and but for this, it would, in all probability, have been now among things which are passed. Having constituted the government, and declared its powers, the people have further said, that since somebody must decide on the extent of these powers, the government shall itself decide—subject always like other popular governments, to its responsibility to the people. And now, sir, I repeat, how is it that a State legislature acquires any right to interfere? Who, or what, gives them the right to say to the people, 'We, who are your agents and servants for one purpose, will undertake to decide, that your other agents and servants, appointed by you for another purpose, have transcended the authority you gave them?' The reply would be, I think, not impertinent, 'Who made you a judge over another's servants. To their own masters they stand or fall.'"

He then went on to show that a State could not make treason against the United States legal, and, says he, when I maintain these sentiments, I am but asserting the rights of the people; I state what they have declared and insisted on as their right to declare it. They have chosen to repose this power in the general government, and I think it my duty to support it like other Constitutional powers.

In referring to the importance of having but one tribunal, whose decisions should be final—Sir, said he:

"If we look to the general nature of the case, could any thing have been more preposterous than to have made a government for the whole Union, and yet left its powers subject, not to one interpretation, but to thirteen or twenty-four interpretations? Instead of one tribunal, established by all, responsible to all, with power to decide for all, shall constitutional questions be left to four and twenty popular bodies, each at liberty to decide for itself, and none bound to respect the decisions of others; and each at liberty, too, to give a new construction, on every new election of its own members? Would any thing, with such a principle in it, or rather with such a destitution of all principle, be fit to be called a government? No, sir. It should not be denominated a constitution. It should be called, rather, a collection of topics for everlasting controversy; heads of debate for a disputatious people. It would not be a government. It would not be adequate to any practical good, nor fit for any people to live under."

Mr. Hayne, already overborne with the overwhelming and unanswerable arguments, was yet destined to receive the most cutting rebuke from his vanquisher. Mr. Webster said:

"And now, Mr. President, let me run the honorable gentleman's doctrine a little into its practical application. Let us look at his probable *modus operandi*. If a thing can be done, an ingenious man can tell *how* it is to be done. Now, I wish to be informed *how* this State interference is to be put in practice. We will take the existing case of the tariff law. South Carolina is said to have made up her opinion upon it. If we do not repeal it, (as probably we shall not,) she will then apply to the case the remedy of her doctrine. She will, we must suppose, pass a law of her legislature, declaring the

several acts of congress, usually called the tariff laws, null
and void, so far as they respect South Carolina, or the citizens
thereof. So far, all is a paper transaction, and easy enough.
But the collector at Charleston is collecting the duties imposed by these tariff laws—he, therefore, must be stopped.
The collector will sieze the goods if the tariff duties are not
paid. The State authorities will undertake their rescue: the
marshal, with his posse, will come to the collector's aid; and
here the contest begins. The militia of the State will be
called out to sustain the nullifying act. They will march,
sir, under a very gallant leader; for I believe the honorable
member himself commands the militia of that part of the
State. He will raise the *nullifying act* on his standard, and
spread it out as his banner. It will have a preamble, bearing that the tariff laws are palpable, deliberate, and dangerous violations of the constitution. He will proceed, with his
banner flying, to the custom house in Charleston—

> " all the while
> Sonorous metal blowing martial sounds."

Arrived at the custom house, he will tell the collector that he
must collect no more duties under any of the tariff laws.
This he will be somewhat puzzled to say, by the way, with a
grave countenance, considering what hand South Carolina
herself had in that of 1816. But, sir, the collector would,
probably, not desist at his bidding. Here would ensue a
pause; for they say, that a certain stillness precedes the tem-
pest. Before this military array should fall on custom house,
collector, clerks, and all, it is very probable some of those
composing it would request of their gallant commander-in-
chief to be informed a little upon the point of law; for they
have doubtless a just respect for his opinions as a lawyer, as
well as for his bravery as a soldier. They know he has read
Blackstone and the constitution, as well as Turenne and Vau-
ban. They would ask him, therefore, something concerning
their rights in this matter. They would inquire whether it
was not somewhat dangerous to resist a law of the United
States. What would be the nature of their offence, they
would wish to learn, if they, by military force and array, re-

sisted the execution in Carolina of a law of the United
States, and it should turn out, after all, that the law *was constitutional.* He would answer, of course, treason. No lawyer could give any other reason. John Fries,* he would tell
them, had learned that some years ago. How, then, they
would ask, do you propose to defend us? We are not afraid
of bullets, but treason has a way of taking people off that
we do not much relish. How do you propose to defend us?
'Look at my floating banner,' he would reply; 'see there the
nullifying law!' Is it your opinion, gallant commander, they
would then say, that if we should be indicted for treason,
that some floating banner of yours would make a good plea
in bar? 'South Carolina is a sovereign State,' he would reply. That is true; but would the judge admit our plea?
'These tariff laws,' he would repeat, 'are unconstitutional,
palpably, deliberately, dangerously.' That all may be so;
but if the tribunals should not happen to be of that opinion,
shall we swing for it? We are ready to die for our country,
but it is rather an awkward business, this dying without
touching the ground. After all, this is a sort of *hemp-*tax,
worse than any part of the tariff.

"Mr. President, the honorable gentleman would be in a
dilemma like that of another great general. He would have
a knot before him which he could not untie. He must cut it
with his sword. He must say to his followers, defend yourselves with your bayonets; and this is war—civil war."

Mr. Webster continued to show that to resist by force the
execution of a law of the United States was treason, and that
the Courts of the United States could take no notice of a
State law to authorize persons to commit that grave crime.
Said he, the common saying that a State cannot commit treason herself, is nothing to the purpose. Can it authorize others
to do so? If John Fries* had produced an act of Pennsylva-

---

* John Fries was a noted leader in what was called the Whisky Rebellion, which became so formidable in 1794 that President Washington issued a proclamation exhorting all persons to desist from any proceedings
tending to prevent the execution of the laws. This did not have the desired effect, however, and it became necessary for the President to order

nia annulling the law of Congress, would it have helped his case? Talk about it as we will, these doctrines go the whole length of revolution. They are incompatible with any peaceable administration of the government. They lead directly to disunion and civil commotion, and therefore it is, that at the commencement, when they are first found to be maintained by respectable men, and in a tangible form, that I enter my protest against them all. Mr Webster proceeded to show that the people of the United States have not chosen the State authorities as their guardians against encroachments from the general government. Said he:

"Sir, the people have not trusted their safety, in regard to the general constitution, to these hands. They have required other security, and taken other bonds. They have chosen to trust themselves, first to the plain words of the instrument, and to such construction as the government, itself, in doubtful cases, should put on its own powers, under their oaths of office, and subject to their responsibility to them; just as the people of a State trust their own State governments with a similar power. Secondly, they have reposed their trust in the efficacy of frequent elections, and in their own power to remove their own servants and agents, whenever they see cause. Thirdly, they have reposed trust in the judicial power, which, in order that it might be trustworthy, they have made as respectable, as disinterested, and as independent as practicable. Fourthly, they have seen fit to rely, in case of necessity, or high expediency, on their known and admitted power to alter or amend the constitution, peaceably and quietly, whenever experience shall point out defects or imperfections. And finally, the people of the United States have

---

out a strong force, numbering some 15,000 men. This argument seemed conclusive and convincing to the rebels of that day, consequently they returned to their several avocations, and by this means quiet was restored. But at that time, as well at the present, there were numerous sympathizers with the traitors, which created a strong and powerful party against the administration of General Washington; but he knew his whole duty, and performed it unhesitatingly, regardless of the denunciations of those who were ever ready to excuse the turbulent for committing treason.

at no time, in no way, directly or indirectly, authorized any State legislature to construe or interpret *their* instrument of government; much less to interfere, by their own power, to arrest its course and operation.

"If, sir, the people in these respects had done otherwise than they have done their constitution could neither have been preserved nor would it have been worth preserving. And if its plain provisions shall now be disregarded, and these new doctrines interpolated in it, it will become as feeble and helpless a being as enemies, whether early or more recent, could possibly desire. It will exist, in every State, but as a poor dependent on State permission. It must borrow leave to be, and will be no longer than State pleasure, or State discretion sees fit to grant the indulgence and to prolong its poor existence.

"But, sir, although there are fears, there are hopes also. The people have preserved this their own chosen Constitution for forty years, and seen their happiness, prosperity and renown grow with its growth, and strengthen with its strength. They are now generally strongly attached to it. Overthrown by direct assault, it cannot be; evaded, undermined, *nullified* it will not be, if we and those who succeed us here, as agents and representatives of the people shall conscientiously and vigilantly discharge the two great branches of our public trust faithfully to preserve and wisely to administer it."

We believe that after perusing the evidence already advanced, every reasonable, unprejudiced person must come to the conclusion that the fathers of our country established the government of the United States with the full understanding and intent that it should be supreme, so far as its delegated authority extended. That it was a unit and capable of sustaining itself by force, if necessary. Mr. Madison's views are repeatedly expressed on this point, explaining the advantages of conferring sufficient powers upon the general government to enable it to suppress internal violence and insurrection, thus providing against the civil commotion that had overthrown other republics of a weaker and less binding obligation on the part of the members composing them. See pages 24, 25 and 26 of this book. The papers here referred to are the more important on account of being written while the question of adoption or rejection of the Constitution was being discussed before the people. Again, on pages 30 to 32, the defects and imperfections of the old confederation in relation to the principles of legislation for the States in their collective capacities, showing more fully that the intention was to create a *government for the people of the United States* that should be binding on all persons, or combination of persons, for all time to come. And again, on page 34, is another quotation from the joint production of Madison, Jay and Hamilton, showing that the government was expected to reach individuals without the aid, and independent of, State authority. And still another quotation, on pages 35 and 36, goes to show that there was a full understanding that the people were conferring certain powers upon the general government, and of course taking them from the States for the purpose of forming one great, inseparable and indissoluble nation. There is not a particle of evidence to prove that the people contemplated reserving or recognizing any State distinction or State sovereignty, so far as the powers of the general government were concerned; but the whole drift of evidence goes to show that they were conscious of the necessity of uniting themselves under one grand government, making themselves one people, reserving only to the States or themselves such powers as were thought necessary to regulate their local affairs, leaving the States in nearly the same relation to the general government that a city municipality is to the government of the State in which it is located; but all must owe obedience to the government of the United States.

But this is not all the evidence we have on this subject. As we review the history of the government, we find that Washington, Jackson, Webster, Clay, and in fact nearly every statesman of any prominence in our political history have either by their acts or words committed themselves to this same policy. The proclamation of General Jackson, and the extracts given of Mr. Webster's arguments, are the key-stone to the arch; they are both conclusive in themselves, and comment by me would be but a weak advocate of their mas- terly and unanswerable arguments, hence I close the subject, conscious of having proven to the satisfaction of myself at least, and, I trust, to some of my doubting Democrtic friends and weak-hearted Republican brethren, that we at least have a government, established by our forefathers, constituting us one nation, one people, with one common country and desti- ny. Whether we shall be found brave enough to defend it and perpetuate it is a question which the God of nations only knows, and time alone will reveal to man.

THE UNION.

Shall this Union be maintained, or shall it be dissolved? are questions that are the all absorbing topics of conversation amongst all classes of people, through the length and breadth of our entire country. There seems to be a great lack of firmness and decision at this time, in relation to the proper course to be pursued in view of the momentous question now about to be presented, discussed and decided upon by the American people.

While true men are thus dumfounded and amazed; I might say silenced with almost a paralyzing astonishment at the daring and rapid movements of the internal enemies to our country; the eyes of the civilized world are turned towards us, and every true friend of liberty and human progression is awaiting our decision upon this grave question, with an almost breathless suspense. In view of this state of things, what course shall we pursue in order to acquit ourselves honarably and preserve our nation from the ruin that seems threatening to blot out the only guarantee that there is such a government as "The United States?" There can be but one answer to this from every true American patriot, and that is, that every attempt to break up this government, let it come from few or many, will be met, be the consequences what they may. The *integrity* of this Union must and shall be maintained, should be the watch-word of every man, woman and child that values the blessing of liberty under which we have prospered as individuals and as a nation. It is contended by some that it is better to allow those States that choose to secede to go in peace than to enter into a civil war, the end of which no man can foretell. This would look very plausible were it not that there is a principle at stake which is at the very foundation of every Demo-

6

cratic government, and without the maintenance of this vital principle self-government is but a farce and a deception. And what is this principle? Why it is nothing more nor less than compelling the minority to submit to the constitutional acts of the majority. Now, who will pretend that a Democratic government can be sustained without this principle is both recognized and, if necessary, enforced?

I am not one of those who think that the question of slavery is the great and only cause of our present troubles; far from it, you may banish every vestige of slavery from our country, and other differences of opinion will rise up, and cause other disputes equally as difficult to settle. Nor is the extent of our country, or the variety of the climate to be charged with our difficulties, for even in our city and State elections we find there is a wide difference of opinion, which results in crimination and recrimination. The same will be found in the various school districts and in many of the churches. Where ever there is a government there must and will be a difference of opinion. It is not to be expected that we will all agree in relation to the various schemes that are presented from time to time for our consideration. But shall we revolt and overthrow the government because our pet scheme is defeated? If not, then should we allow others to involve us in one common ruin because of their defeat? There would be no end to this rebellious spirit if the obligation to submit to a constitutional election was removed. What would be the result of giving way to those who are now threatening our peace? Would not every other community have the same right; and we having once granted the right by allowing a portion of the nation to set up an independent government, how could we in justice punish those who choose to go and do likewise? State governments will have the same difficulty to contend against that the United States have now, and instead of strength and prosperity we will be weak and divided and without honor at home or abroad.

I think that every sane man will agree with me when I say that it is much better to meet on one grand battle field and settle this question at once than to dodge the responsibility for the present, only to allow dissention to spread broad cast over the land. When this great nation has been torn into fragments by this ranting, ungovernable spirit, we, or our children, will have to enforce this great principle, that some of our best meaning friends are willing to abandon for the sake of peace.

THE EFFECT OF A WAR TO SUSTAIN OUR GOVERNMENT.

The effect of a war to sustain our government would be to plant the seed of true patriotism in the breast of every law-abiding and liberty-loving citizen of America. We should be able to contrast the two extremes of our unheard of prosperity and the miseries and horrors of civil war—which of itself would do much towards insuring peace for centuries to come. Let those who expect that we love peace so well, or dread war so much as to allow them to bid defiance to all laws, learn that they are mistaken; that we are not the degenerate sons of a noble ancestry, but knowing our rights and loving our country, we are determined to defend them against every encroachment, and we will hear no more threats about disunion or rebellion in consequence of a political defeat. We shall then have established beyond a controversy that the minority must and shall submit to the constitutional acts of the majority. We will then have established in the minds of the civilized world that our government is not one of straw, but that it is not only capable of vindicating its honor in defiance of foreign foes, but it is equally able to chastise those who rebel against its authority at home. War would be to our political system, what the thunderstorm is to the atmosphere. Its purifying influences would be manifested by inspiring new life, vigor and purity into everything that surrounds us. Political demagogues will be cast aside as unfit for public confidence, and better and more patriotic men will spring up from among the masses who will have before them the history of the troubles through which their country has passed as lesson and a warning to shun a like calamity.

We have heretofore shown ourselves to be equal to our undertakings, and now when the great crisis in our national affairs is at hand, and the eyes of the friends of liberty throughout the civilized world are gazing upon us with the deepest anxiety, shall we be found unworthy of the liberties we enjoy? Should we be found unfaithful to the trust imposed on us by our forefathers? We would be the just object of scorn and contempt, and the historian who shall undertake the task of writing the true history of the rise and fall of the American government, will have the painful duty of drawing the contrast between the noble and patriotic heroes who established it, and the cowardly, selfish and unprincipled traitors who became its destroyers.

SHALL THE PEOPLE RULE?

This question is frequently asked by those who are encouraging the Southern rebellion. I answer, most emphatically, in the affirmative. But let us see who the people are. It is plain that the people of a State are not those of one or more of the counties, unless the people of those counties are a majority of all the people in the State. Now the Constitution of the United States comes from the people of all the States, consequently it will be perceived that they alone and not the people of one State have the right to alter or abolish it. As well might the people of Indianapolis declare the Constitution of the the State of Indiana null and void, as for the people of one State to declare this Union dissolved. It is true that men talk about "States' rights," "the equality of the States," and in fact invent every manner of argument for the purpose of shielding those who are committing treason against the government of the United States, but where is the clause of the constitution that discloses any such sentiments? There is none, but on the other hand we find the most positive proof that the framers of that article intended that we should be one great nation, and to secure us against the liability of sudden and unnecessary changes they provided that in order to amend the constitution the consent of three-fourths of all the States were necessary, hence it will be perceived that a simple majority of the people of the United States could not amend the constitution, much less declare it null and void.

In view of this wise provision so necessary to secure stability to our government, how rediculous it is to talk about a single State declaring this Union dissolved against the well-known wish of four-fifths of all the people of our entire country. The thing is absurd in the extreme and should not be entertained for a moment, for such a principle once established would be the end of all constitutional governments. But suppose we grant the independence of such States as choose to withdraw from the Union. In order to do this we must amend the constitution so as to empower Congress to act upon the matter, and until then, every member of Congress is bound to stand by the constitution as it is, for there is no power granted them to treat with a portion of this nation as an independent sovereign power. The framers of the Constitution did not grant Congress any more than a State the right to dismember or dissolve the Union. And who would for a moment consent to the assumption of such extraordinary and important authority by those who were sent to Washington to support the very constitution which they are now called upon to disregard and destroy.

WHAT SHOULD THE PEOPLE DO TO AVERT THE THREATENING STORM?

In my opinion, the best way to stop this disunion and treasonable clamor, is for all friends of the Union to come out and call meetings, and pass resolutions such as are appropriate for the times, telling our enemies that it was for this Union our fathers fought, bled and died, and we will do (if necessary) as our fathers did. Let there be but one sentiment, and the unbroken ranks of eighteen millions of freemen will do more to silence treason than all the constitutional amendments that could be prepared by twice the number of pacificators that are now offering their services to induce the government to meet the traitors on what is termed "middle ground." It is this continued wavering and uncertain position of the people that give those who are plotting our destruction such full and perfect confidence in their final success. Few men could be found who would enter the enemies ranks, if the certainty of being dealt with according to the laws of our country was before them. The boasted bravery of those chivalrous gentlemen who are now firing the hearts of the ignorant with bitter hatred against the noblest government on earth, would hesitate, reflect, and recoil at the sight of the hangman and the gallows. I question not their bravery, neither do I doubt their determination, but with the certainty of defeat before them, would they strike the fatal blow? Every sane man is apt to count the chances of success when he enters upon any very important undertaking, and if there is nothing before him but humiliation and defeat, where is the man who would be found fool hardy enough to risk his life in such a hopeless enterprise? They are few and far between. We are told that unless the nation gives way to these traitors, that the war that will ensue will be the most bloody and desperate ever known to civilized man. There is no doubt but they will fight, but will they be found any more brave and determined in destroying than we will be in maintaining our glorious country? I presume not. Then we can easily discovery the character of the war by deciding upon the course we would pursue in such a contingency. This talk about such a war being any worse than other wars, is a mere bugbear, sent out to frighten the timid into submission, and the less notice there is taken of it, the more unfrequent will it be referred to. It is a noticable fact, that those who are bringing about this great calamity are the very ones who are picturing to our visions the horrible consequences that would result from an effort to stop their career. Can impudence go further? Could Arnold have done more to have accomplished his base and ignoble purpose?

Then let the friends of our country rally under its banner, and then and there resolve anew to stand by this Union as the only safety for our peace, our prosperity, and our liberties. There should be no partizan prejudice, for it is not the question who shall rule the country, but whether we shall have a country to rule. We all have a common interest in preserving this government, and none should wait for this or that politician, for they are all waiting to see the determination of the people before they will take a very decided stand.

Nor can the politicians alone save our country. Far from it. They are the parties who aided in bringing about our present political troubles which are threatening to involve us in a deadly contest to save our country from dissolution. As well might you prescribe arsenic and expect it to cure a patient who was threatened with death from the excessive use of that poisonous drug, as to look to the politicians to restore peace and prosperity to our distracted country.

Since it is the people that must save our country, if saved at all, let there be unanimity, firmness and decision upon the all important question of preserving the Union; not if we can carry out our pet scheme; not if South Carolina is willing. Neither should we make any other condition, but resolve unalterably to stand by the constitution and the laws to the end, and never for one moment think of abandoning our undertaking, until this noble object shall have been accomplished. It is a duty that we owe to ourselves, to our homes and firesides, to the friends of freedom throughout the civilized world, to those who are plotting treason against our government, and to the God of liberty, that we should speak out plainly and to the point, and warn those who are expecting such an easy victory, that they are sadly and seriously mistaken; that we are not, as has been represented to them, divided, but we are as one man for our country, unconditionally and unalterably, and though we may differ in relation to the policy of conducting the great ship of state, yet we will not abandon her, nor allow others to commit depredations against her. The people of this great nation will never consent to a peaceable destruction of this noble fabric. Never! never! no, never! Then should we not warn those who are expecting an easy victory, against the awful consequences of a persistence in their destructive policy? By our silence we encourage them, by our inactivity we strengthen them, and by our indecision we give them confidence. The policy to be pursued should be distinctly laid down and presented to them. They have been deceived and encouraged with the prospect of success by the course we have pursued, and should war become necessary in order to enforce the laws, we are culpable, in a measure, for not showing more firmness at an earlier period. There is no room to doubt their determination to bid defiance to the constitution and the laws of the land, and nothing short of a show of the ability and the determination to stand by our country, will induce them to desist. It may now be too late to avoid bloodshed, but the sooner the remedy the less severe will be the calamity.

We are told that to stir this matter up at the north will only excite and spread the feeling of dissatisfaction more swiftly over the land, but the time has come when, to my mind, we must prepare to decide between our national existence or non-existence. And should we be afraid of offending the enemies of our country? Those who would turn against the government, provided their peculiar notions in relation to some particular question is rejected, are against the whole spirit of a democratic government, and will be found against us in the end, and we may as well count them there first as last. A submission to their dictation would be to yield the reins of government into the hands of those who are determined to either rule or ruin, which must evidently result in the latter.

Let us examine the bearing of this rule or ruin policy, and see where it would end, provided we give way to those who choose to adopt it. I know of no better example, to test its destructiveness, than the one presented to us in the present unsettled condition of our country. The people have elected a President and Vice President in strict conformity with the provisions of the constitution, made and provided for that purpose. Of this there is no dispute. There is no use in talking about the issue being sectional, for every person who was legally entitled to vote for President and Vice President of the United States, and who concurred with the sentiments of the party, was invited to take part in the election. There was no distinction between North and South in this matter, and the plea set forth that there was no support from one-half of the country, does not alter the case, especially since it is well known that the political opponents of Mr. Lincoln would not allow the free discussion of the various issues presented to the people for their consideration. Had this course been pursued in the North, there would not have been a Breckenridge party in many of the Northern States. It will be perceived, that owing to this intolerant spirit exhibited in some portions of the South, Mr. Lincoln's views were not, and could not be presented to the people for their consideration, which is in itself entirely inconsistent with the spirit of a free government, as well as a violation of the constitution and laws of our country. But who was to blame for this spirit of mobocracy? Was it Mr. Lincoln or his friends? Nothing but a bigoted blindness could lead any reasonable and well informed man to an affirmative conclusion. The simple fact that Mr. Yancey, the leader of the most ultra opponents of the Republicans, was allowed to advocate his views all over the North without molestation or even insult, proves to the contrary. But we are told that the Republican principles are contrary to Southern interests. What if they are? Is that a reason why the right of free discussion should be blotted out of existence? The principles of Mr. Yancey are thought by a large majority of the people of the free States, to be *decidedly* against the interest of the whole country.

But did they propose to destroy this government if Mr. Breckenridge was elected? Did they insult him, or drive him from the country as a felon? No, he was kindly treated and listened to. The people, however, did not conclude to vote his principles, and for this they are treated as criminals of the deepest dye. *Comment is unnecessary.* But supposing Mr. Breckenridge had been elected, and Massachusetts had placed herself in the unenviable position that South Carolina has assumed, where is the statesman who would have advocated the justice of her position, or her right to secede, and thereby break up this government, unless Mr. Breckenridge would renounce his doctrine, and propose a change in the constitution recognizing the Republican principles, and who would be found willing to compromise the honor and dignity of the government by conceding to such demands? If any there be who would lend their aid to such a scheme, they are mere political demagogues without honor, and are not entitled to the confidence of the people. In this, I presume, nearly every person will agree with me. Still, when we turn to the South, there seems to be some diversity of opinion in relation to what course should be pursued. Now, why this difference? Can it be charged to anything but political prejudices? True patriotism never begets such inconsistencies.

Now it is plain that if any party make it a condition that they must be allowed to control this government, in order to allow us to live in peace, then that party, above all things, should not be allowed such control. The mere demand shows the incompetency of such party to occupy such an important position in our national affairs. Suppose we should grant the present request. Are we prepared to grant the next that may be made at any future time? If so, tell me, if you please, when and where you will be willing to make a stand for the vindication of our constitutional rights? Are we to give way to one demand after another until we have transferred all the rights which we now possess to this rule or ruin party?

It is contended by some that, by allowing those States which desire to secede from this Union, to go without opposition, it will insure us peace, and at the same time remove the slave question from congress, and, thereby, our political troubles are at an end. Happy man is he who can imagine such a political millennium so near at hand, and so easily to be obtained. I would ask whether other questions may not come up that will divide the people, and cause the same bitter feeling that now distracts the whole country when another section will demand a separation from the remaining States; and whether they will not have the same right that we are now called upon to grant to the Cotton States? It is plain to me that if this policy, of allowing any State to secede that can raise a pretext for doing so, is to be adopted. we will soon have no government at all; but in the place of this law-abiding and liberty loving community, where peace, plenty and prosperity has smiled upon us so many happy years, anarchy will reign, with all its blasting and withering influences, laying waste our brightest hopes, and casting a gloom and dispair over everything that has heretofore been the pride of every true American citizen. We are now called upon to consent to divide this nation under the penalty of

civil war; the horrors of which we all deeply deplore, and
are willing to prevent by all reasonable measures. But, can
we grant what is asked without establishing a precedent that
will lead to further demands, and a consequent sub-division,
and, in fact, division after division until this glorious and
prosperous country shall be (instead of one great, powerful
and honored nation,) thirty-three petty contending States,
each striving to get the advantage of the other? It is contended by some that, by making concessions, both war and dissolution can be prevented. But, let us look at their character,
and the circumstances under which they are demanded, and
see whether such results, under existing circumstances, are
likely to be realized.

The people of the United States have just cast their votes
in accordance with the usages and customs heretofore adopted,
as well as in perfect conformity with their constitutional
rights, and, as usual in such cases, there has been more than
one party. The result has been that one party elected their
choice, while the others were necessarily unsuccessful; and
instead of submitting, like true patriots, peaceably to the
constitutional acts of the people, a portion of the defeated
party demand of those who have, by their numbers, carried
the election, the surrender of their principles. This is the
basis of the compromise that the freemen of this nation are
unblushingly asked to make. But, upon inquiry as to whether said conditional rebels (for they are nothing else) are willing to aid in suppressing the more ultra and unconditional
rebels of such States that have already declared themselves out
of the Union, we find them bitterly opposed to everything
that tends to show the supremacy of the laws over this
traitorous secession dogma; and our candid opinion is, that
every individual who places himself upon this platform, is
contemplating a deep laid scheme for the purpose of obtaining all the public territory they possibly can for the institution of slavery, and then withdraw from the Union with
their booty. Ask them if they are willing to submit in case
the people reject their demands, and the answer is, no, they
will die first. Thus the ultimatum is presented to us to either

surrender our principles, our country, or fight to sustain it.
Fellow-countrymen we need not ask you which you will do.

Let us sift this unparalleled scheme of impudence and see
whether it is going to be productive of permanent good
to any one except to those who are desirous of involving us
in anarchy and ruin.

Supposing the Republicans should abandon their principles, which seem to be the terms upon which peace is offered.
and, in 1864, the Democrats should succeed in electing the
President upon the slave-extension platform, and the Republicans, feeling that their interests were likely to be trampled
upon by the dominant party, should say to the Democracy that,
unless said Democrats would abandon the principles of their
party, and secure the Republicans against the exercise of
their principles in the future, by an amendment to the constitution itself, they (the Republicans) would dissolve this
Union? It will be observed that, if one party has the right
to demand concessions, the other party has the same right,
consequently it would not be the majority that would rule,
but the minority. Neither have we any guarantee that, by
granting the present demands, that other and still more absurd and threatening demands will not be made. We are
now called upon to incorporate into the constitution certain
additional rights and privileges for slavery ; and what is the
threatened penalty that is offered to the freemen of this nation if they fail to grant what is demanded? Why it is
nothing less than a complete overthrow and destruction of
this government—and yet the Republicans are taunted with
the charge of being the cause of all the consequences of the
great calamity that seems awaiting our destruction. I call
especial attention to this subject, more particularly in consequence of the probable effort that will be made to force what
is called the "Crittenden Amendment," upon the people. It
should be remembered that Mr. Crittenden proposes, not only
to give all the territory south of 36° 30′ to the slave interests, but all the territory hereafter acquired.

The restoration of the Missouri Compromise sounds very
smooth and pleasant to the ear, but is it the Missouri Compromise that Mr. Crittenden proposes to restore? Far from

it. Let us look at the broad difference between the two measures, and see whether there is not something that looks as though there was deception, of the deepest dye, about to be practiced upon those who are desirous of preserving the territories free from the blighting curse of slavery. We have heard much about the Missouri Compromise, also about Mr. Crittendon's amendment, and, for the benefit of those who are not familiar with the two measures, we will give them both in full. The following is all that relates to the institution of slavery in what is called the Missouri Compromise :

"SEC. 8. *And be it further enacted,* That, in all the territory ceded by France to the United States, under the name of Louisiana, which lies north of thirty-six degrees and thirty minutes north latitude, not included within the limits of the State contemplated by this act, (meaning Missouri,) slavery and involuntary servitude, otherwise than in the punishment of crime, whereof the parties shall have been duly convicted, shall be and is hereby forever prohibited ; provided, always, that any person escaping into the same, from whom service is lawfully claimed in any State or Territory of the United States, such fugitive may be lawfully re-claimed and conveyed to the person claiming his or her services as aforesaid."

It will be perceived that the above section does not establish slavery anywhere, but, on the contrary, it prohibited it in all the territory north of 36° 30′ north latitude, while south of that (we can only infer for there is nothing explicit on the subject) the people were to have slavery or not as they might decide amongst themselves. But, in order to the more fully understanding the effect of the Missouri Compromise, it is necessary to know the amount of territory belonging, at that time, to the United States, lying south of said above mentioned line. The territory that now constitutes the State of Arkansas, and a small tract of Indian territory, which now belongs to four tribes of Indians, to-wit: the Chickasaws, Seminoles, Cherokees, and Choctaws, all of which territory, including that of Arkansas, is not much larger than the State of Missouri, was all the territory that remained of the Louisiana purchase, belonging to the United States, south of 36° 30′ north latitude, at the time of the passage of said compromise. How different, in effect, from the above is the Crittenden amendment. Let us see. The following is the said amendment that is harped about as being a restoration of the Missouri Compromise. Read and behold the difference:

"WHEREAS, Serious and alarming dissensions have arisen between the Northern and Southern States, concerning the rights and security of the rights of slaveholding States, and especially their rights in the common territory of the United States; and whereas, it is eminently desirable and proper that these dissensions, which now threaten the very existence of this Union, should be permanently quieted and settled by constitutional provisions, which shall do equal justice to all sections, and thereby restore to the people that peace and good will which ought to prevail between all the citizens of the United States: Therefore,

"*Resolved by the Senate and House of Representatives of the United States of America in Congress assembled,* (two-thirds of both houses concurring,) That the following articles be, and are hereby proposed and submitted as amendments to the Constitution of the United States, which shall be valid to all intents and purposes, as part of said Constitution, when ratified by conventions of three-fourths of the several States:

"ART. 1. In all the territory of the United States now held, or hereafter acquired, situated north of latitude 36 deg. 30 min., slavery or involuntary servitude, except as a punishment for crime, is prohibited while such territory shall remain under territorial government. In all the territory south of said line of latitude, slavery of the African race is hereby recognized as existing, and shall not be interfered with by Congress, but shall be protected as property by all the departments of the territorial government during its continuance. And when any territory, north or south of said line, within such boundaries as Congress may prescribe, shall contain the population requisite for a member of Congress according to the then federal ratio of representation of the people of the United States, it shall, if its form of government be republican, be admitted into the Union, on an equal footing with the original States, with or without slavery, as the constitution of such new State may provide.

"Art. 2. Congress shall have no power to abolish slavery in places under its exclusive jurisdiction, and situate within the limits of States that permit the holding of slaves.

"Art. 3. Congress shall have no power to abolish slavery within the District of Columbia, so long as it exists in the adjoining States of Virginia and Maryland, or either, nor without the consent of the inhabitants, nor without just compensation first made to such owners of slaves as do not consent to such abolishment. Nor shall Congress at any time prohibit officers of the Federal Government, or members of Congress, whose duties require them to be in said District, from bringing with them their slaves, and holding them as such during the time their duties may require them to remain there, and afterwards taking them from the District.

"Art. 4. Congress shall have no power to prohibit or hinder the transportation of slaves from one State to another, or to a Territory, in which slaves are permitted to be held, whether that transportation be by land, navigable rivers, or by sea.

"Art. 5. That in addition to the provisions of the third paragraph of the second section of the fourth article of the Constitution of the United States, Congress shall have power to provide by law, and it shall be its duty so to provide, that the United States shall pay to the owner who shall apply for it, the full value of his fugitive slave in all cases when the Marshal or other officer, whose duty it was to arrest said fugitive, was prevented from so doing by violence, or when, after arrest, said fugitive was rescued by force, and the owner thereby prevented and obstructed in the pursuit of his remedy for the recovery of his fugitive slave under the said clause of the Constitution and the laws made in pursuance thereof. And in all such cases, when the United States shall pay for such fugitive, they shall have the right, in their own name, to sue the county in which said violence, intimidation, or rescue was committed, and to recover from it, with interest and damages, the amount paid by them for said fugitive slave. And

the said county, after it has paid said amount to the United
States, may, for its indemnity, sue and recover from the wrong
doers or rescuers, by whom the owner was prevented from
the recovery of his fugitive slave, in like manner as the owner himself might have sued and recovered.

"ART. 6. No future amendment to the Constitution shall
affect the five preceding articles; nor the third paragraph of
the second section of the first article of the Constitution;
and no amendment shall be made to the Constitution which
shall authorize or give to Congress any power to abolish or
interfere with slavery in any of the States by whose law it
is, or may be, allowed or permitted.

And whereas, also, beside those causes of dissension em-
braced in the foregoing amendments proposed to the Constitution of the United States, there are others which come within the jurisdiction of Congress, and may be remedied by its
legislative power; and whereas it is the desire of Congress,
as far as its power will extend, to remove all just cause for
the popular discontent and agitation which now disturb the
peace of the country, and threaten the stability of its institutions: Therefore,

"1. *Resolved by the Senate and House of Representatives of
the United States of America, in Congress assembled,* That the
laws now in force, for the recovery of fugitives, are in strict
pursuance of the plain and mandatory provisions of the constitution, and have been sanctioned as valid and constitutional
by the judgment of the Supreme Court of the United States:
that the slaveholding States are entitled to the faithful observance and execution of those laws, and that they ought
not to be repealed, or so modified or changed as to impair
their efficiency; and that laws ought to be made for the punishment of those who attempt, by rescue of the slave. or
other illegal means, to hinder or defeat the due execution of
said laws.

"2. That all State laws which conflict with the fugitive
slave acts of congress, or any other constitutional acts of congress, or which in their operation impede, hinder or delay
the free course and due execution of any of said acts, are null
and void by the plain provisions of the constitution of the

United States; yet those State laws, void as they are, have given color to practices, and led to consequences, which have obstructed the due administration and execution of acts of congress and especially the acts for the delivery of fugitive slaves, and have thereby contributed much to the discord and commotion now prevailing. Congress, therefore, in the present perilous juncture, does not deem it improper respectfully and earnestly to recommend the repeal of those laws to the several States which have enacted them, or such legislative corrections and explanations of them as may prevent their being used or perverted to such mischievous purposes.

"3. That the act of the 18th of September, 1850, commonly called the fugitive slave law, ought to be so amended as to make the fee of the commissioner, mentioned in the 8th section of the act, equal in amount, in the cases decided by him, whether his decision be in favor of or against the claimant. And to avoid misconstruction, the last clause of the 5th section of said act, which authorises the person holding the warrant for the arrest or detention of a fugitive slave, to summon to his aid the *posse comitatus*, and which declares it to be the duty of all good citizens to assist him in its execution, ought to be amended so as to expressly limit the authority and duty to cases in which there shall be resistance or danger of resistance or rescue.

"4. That the laws for the suppression of the African slave trade, and especially those prohibiting the importation of slaves in the United States, ought to be made effectual, and ought to be thoroughly executed, and all further enactments necessary to those ends ought to be promptly made."

The above is unblushingly urged upon the people by some portions of the Democracy as being eminently conservative, and, above all, a middle ground, upon which all patriots should be willing to stand or fall for the Union; but as for me I am entirely unable to see that there is any middle ground about it. What can we understand by this proposition? Is it not granting all the South have ever asked? When, and wherein, have they asked more? Could Mr. Yancey himself have made out a stronger document? And yet, we are told that the South are making great concessions when they submit to this measure, and cease to commit treason against the government. In the name of enlightened reason, I ask, could there be a greater insult offered to the free men of this nation, than to demand of them the sanction of the above proposed amendment, and thus engraft it into the Constitution of this government, claiming, as we do, to be the freest government in the world.

Upon an examination of Mr. Crittenden's proposition, it will be perceived that he irrevocably consigns to slavery all the Territory that we now have, or may hereafter acquire, south of thirty-six degrees and thirty minutes, north latitude, and north of that line he leaves the matter for the people to decide when they come to form a State government. By comparing this measure with the Missouri Compromise, it will be perceived that Mr. Crittenden proposes to leave the northern territory in the same condition that the Missouri Compromise left the territory south of said line.

But let us view this beautiful document of Mr. Crittenden's a little further, and see how modestly the people of the free States are asked to pay for Sambo whenever he gets it into his head to emigrate northward, provided some one or more of his sable brethren should chance to advise those whose duty it may be to invite Sambo to return to the "Sunny South," to make tracks with the heels towards the shanty, and allow Sambo to remain where the winters are longer. Yes, we are asked by Mr. C. to pay for Sambo whenever the marshal, whose duty it is to arrest him, is *intimidated*. This sounds most beautiful. Let the people once agree to this and we would soon have the privilege of paying for hundreds of thousands, I might say millions, of the refractory portion of the slave population, and in order to understand these fully, the consequences of adopting Mr. Crittenden's amendment, it will be well for us to estimate the probable number of the slave population in the future, as well as their inclination to escape.

It is a well known fact, that if the slave population should increase for the next eighty years as fast as they have for the past eighty years, they will amount to between forty and fifty millions of inhabitants. Now let us imagine that number of slaves, with the natural increase of intelligence, together with a corresponding decrease of the preponderance of African blood in their veins, and it will not take a very strong imaginative individual to perceive that the number of fugitives will increase at a fearful rate, and to such an extent that it would impoverish the whole nation to pay for them. By a careful examination of Mr. Crittenden's amendment it will be perceived that it provides for recovering the value of the slave, by the United States, of the county in which said violence, INTIMIDATION, or rescue was committed.

Now let us suppose that this should become a part and parcel of the Constitution of the United States, and some one or more of the States should pass laws nullifying said provision, and at the same time demand a revision of the Constitution in such a manner as to annul said clause, as a condition that they would remain in the Union, will our Union-saving friends be willing to meet the case by granting the demand, or will they stand up for the enforcement of the laws and the preservation of the Union? If so, then why not assist in enforcing the laws against South Carolina or any other State that proposes to nullify the Constitution and the laws made in pursuance thereof. Partisan prejudice cannot prevent any person from seeing that if one portion of the people have the right to make a demand for concessions, then any and all other portions are entitled to the exercise of the same right, and where such demands have been complied with in one case, there is no rule whereby they could justly be denied in another. Is there not great danger that by granting the South what they are now demanding, especially since the demand is accompanied with threats of such a grave character, we will establish a precedence that will sap the very principle upon which our government is based? In all Democratic governments it is the duty of every individual to submit to the laws duly enacted by a constitutional majority; and whenever one portion of the people rebel against said laws they become not only traitors to their country but to the very principles upon which self government is founded. In view of this, it is clear to me that to make any concession, under the existing menacing threats, would be to offer a bounty to all future conspirators against the government, and thus endanger the peace of our country for all time to come. Such being the case, why talk about compromises and concessions. Let us enforce obedience to the present government before we talk of compromises. To treat with men who bid defiance to the supreme law of the land, who are now engaged in open and active treason against the government, would be humiliating to every true American citizen, and a disgrace to us as a nation, besides showing to the world the most *positive* evidence of our weakness; but on the other hand let firmness and justice be the order of the day, and although war may ensue let the consequences rest with those who are trying to overthrow this great temple of freedom, and we shall outride the threatend storm and transmit to posterity, unimpaired, this sacred legacy, bequeathed to us by our forefathers and sealed by their blood. We will then have shown ourselves worthy of the free institutions we have inherited, and our children's children will be stimulated by our example to extra exertions to perpetuate and strengthen the bonds that is to preserve this nation in all its destined magnificent grandeur.

In conclusion, let me exhort my fellow-countrymen to stand or fall by our country. Let us not forget that our fathers, as well as we, loved peace and abhorred the calamities of war; and although the most of them have long since "gone to that bourne from which no traveler returns," yet when they were called to their country's service, they were surrounded by all the endearing ties which we now enjoy. Many a son received the mother's last parting blessing, and bid her his last farewell this side of the grave. Husbands bid their wives an affectionate adieu, to meet no more on earth; and many a bitter tear has flown from the weeping eyes of the loved ones in that lonely home, bereft of a father, husband, or brother who has fallen in the deadly struggle for the liberties we have inherited. And should we prove recreant to our trust, the immortal spirits of those noble-hearted, self-sacrificing patriots who fell while struggling with a powerful tyrant in front, and a deadly savage foe in the rear, to gain the freedom

of this our beloved country, would rise up from their graves
and rebuke us for our low, cringing cowardice. No, my fellow-countrymen, you will not be found wanting for courage—
you will not allow this temple of freedom to be destroyed—
you will stand by the Constitution and the Union, and prove
yourselves worthy of your noble ancestry.

AGENTS WANTED

TO INTRODUCE

THE AMERICAN FAMILY PHYSICIAN,

BY JOHN KING, M. D.

PREPARED EXPRESSLY FOR FAMILY USE.

This valuable work is a large, royal octavo volume of nearly 1,200 pages; containing nearly twice as much matter on the subject of health and disease, as can be found in any similar work ever before offered to the American people. Instead of describing diseases and remedies in the mysterious and incomprehensible terms of the profession, the author has used language such as the people understand. No less than *three hundred and seventy forms of disease*, including diseases of women, diseases of children, chronic diseases, as well as those of a surgical nature are accurately described and the most successful methods of treatment made known.

Nearly *five hundred simple medicines are described*, together with their virtues and medicinal uses. And the recipes for some *two hundred and fifty valuable and successful compounds and preparations* are given.

The following are some of the numerous notices and recommendations the work has received by those who have given it an examination.

The following is from the justly celebrated Dr. Burnham, proprietor of the Chronic Disease Infirmary of this city.

INDIANAPOLIS, IND., JAN. 14TH, 1861

A. D. STREIGHT, ESQ.: *Dear Sir*—Having carefully examined a work of your publication entitled, "New American Family Physician," by John King, M. D., I find in point of style that it is concise, couched in plain language, and free from technicalities. Voluminous in variety of topics discussed, it comprises an amount of practical matter pertaining to the preservation of health, the history and treatment of disease unequaled in adaptation for popular use. A more general diffusion of knowledge upon the topics therein discussed, will serve as one of the greatest protections against the intrusions of ignorant pretenders who propose to tamper with human health and life. And I trust will be cordially hailed by every intelligent physician appreciating the fact that the stupid credulity of ignorance is much more forminable to encounter than the wisdom of an enlightened intelligence. In fine, the volume is worthy of the well earned reputation of its author, and I cheerfully commend it as highly deserving a prominent place in the library of every family. Truly yours,

N. G. BURNHAM, M. D.

[*From Dr. G. M. Thompson, Agent for Kansas*]

Tell Dr. King that I have had the pleasure of selling a copy of his "Physician" to Ex-Governor C. Robinson, Ex-Governor F. P. Stanton, Ex-Governor Wilson Shannon, and all the principal men in the Territory, as far as I have been able to canvass.

THE CRISIS

OF

Eighteen Hundred and Sixty-One,

IN THE GOVERNMENT OF THE

UNITED STATES,

ITS CAUSE,

AND HOW IT SHOULD BE MET.

BY A. D. STREIGHT.

The intention of the author in bringing this work before the people at this time, is to promote unity of action in sustaining our country from the dangers that seem threatening to not only destroy our government, but the very principles upon which our liberties are based. And, for the purpose of giving it a wide spread circulation, we have put the wholesale price within a fraction of the cost of manufacturing.

PRICES.—25 cents per single copy; $2.25 per dozen copies; $7.50 for fifty copies, and $12.50 per hundred.

Orders from the friends of the Union, and the trade generally, are solicited, and will receive prompt attention. Address

A. D. STREIGHT,
Indianapolis, Ind.